THE GHOSTMOBILE

Look for these and
other Apple Paperbacks
in your local bookstore!

The Secret Life of Dilly McBean
by Dorothy Haas

The Lemonade Trick
by Scott Corbett

Oh, Brother
by Johnniece Marshall Wilson

Christina's Ghost
by Betty Ren Wright

When the Dolls Woke
by Marjorie Filley Stover

Haunted Island
by Joan Lowery Nixon

THE GHOSTMOBILE

KATHY KENNEDY TAPP

AN
APPLE
PAPERBACK

SCHOLASTIC INC.
New York Toronto London Auckland Sydney

Scholastic Books are available at special discounts for quantity pur-
chases for use as premiums, promotional items, retail sales through
specialty market outlets, etc. For details contact: Special Sales Man-
ager, Scholastic Inc., 730 Broadway, New York, NY 10003.

ISBN 0-590-41582-4

Copyright © 1987 by Kathleen Kennedy Tapp. All rights reserved. Pub-
lished by Scholastic Inc., 730 Broadway, New York, NY 10003, by arrange-
ment with Harper & Row, Publisher's, Inc. APPLE PAPERBACKS is a
registered trademark of Scholastic Inc.

12 11 10 9 8 7 6 5 4 3 2 1   8 9/8 0 1 2 3/9

Printed in the U.S.A.   28

First Scholastic printing, May 1988

To Cathy Norris
and the JPL Children's Department "Gang"

With thanks to Sue and Amy Nelson,
Dan and Sheryl Barrette, and especially
Dean and Mary Lou Einerson

1

Captain's Log: Stardate June 15, Monday:

*Four real kids and one imaginary one
are too many to squeeze into the back
of a Chevette.*

I balanced my logbook carefully on my lap so it didn't
touch Josh's knee on one side or Carrie's knee on the
other side. Then, in my special code writing that left
the loops off the tall letters, I added:

*Especially when the Chevette is going
the wrong way.*

"Are we there yet?" Brooke asked for the twenty-
fifth time.

"No, we still have a way to go," Mom answered for
the twenty-fifth time.

1

"I don't have anything to do!" Brooke's voice was always high and squeaky. Now it was getting blubbery. "And neither does Miss Icicle."

Mom turned around. "Can't one of you kids read to her or something?" She looked at me first. "Ryan?"

"I'm writing in my logbook." I stared down at my lap.

"And I'm reading," Carrie said quickly, hiding behind her *Caddie Woodlawn* book.

"I'm right in the middle of a war." Josh leaned over his electronic space game, madly pushing buttons. "Bam! Twenty points!" Little bleep-bleep-bleeps filled the back seat.

Dad fiddled with the car radio knobs. "Where's the public radio station around here? At a time like this I need Bach or Beethoven."

"When are we going to get there?" Brooke yelled, right in my ear. I pushed her toward Carrie.

"*You* read to her. Read *Caddie Woodlawn*. You won't even have to look at the pages. You must know the whole thing by heart."

"Huh?" She gave me a blank stare, then bent over her book again. I might as well have tried to talk to the windshield wipers.

Carrie is a bookworm-plus. She reads books so fast, she practically inhales them. All kinds. But *Caddie Woodlawn* is her all-time favorite. Reading about a pioneer girl probably makes her feel like she's brave and strong instead of short and scrawny, with stubby braids and chewed-off fingernails. I poked her.

"Doesn't it get kind of boring when you know everything that's going to happen?"

"Shh. I'm right in the best part," she mumbled, still staring at the book.

"Brooke, when you stand there, your head's in the rearview mirror." Dad's voice was very slow and calm. A sure danger signal.

"It is not. It's on my shoulders," Brooke answered, turning around with a grin to see if everyone got her joke.

I groaned. Josh made a barf noise.

"Brooke . . ." Dad warned. "Your head—"

"I can't move over! I can't do anything! If I sit down, I'll get smushed between Josh and Ryan. And Miss Icicle won't have any room. And . . . and . . . my wart hurts." She sniffed loudly.

"Dummy, warts don't hurt."

"*Mine* does." She held her finger up to my face so I could see her wart sticking out below her knuckle like a stubby, flesh-colored nail. Ever since the doctor said it had to come off, she'd been acting like a wounded soldier. "And I have to go to the bathroom and—"

"Sing," Mom said loudly. "Sing us a song, Brooke."

"*No!*" Josh yelped, covering his ears. "I can't take it!"

"Mom, what did you tell her that for?" I cried. "Now we'll all have to listen to her dumb songs the whole rest of the trip!"

"Would you rather read her your logbook?" Mom asked softly, with a look that could have deflected an enemy laser beam.

Brooke smiled, her tears instantly gone.

"Nah nah na-na-na! Nah na-na-na!" she sang loudly, in her best country western nasal twang. She strummed her fingers across the front of her T-shirt.

Carrie slammed her book shut. "It's impossible to concentrate in this car!" she cried.

Mom ran her hand through her hair. "Brooke, do you know any nursery school songs?"

Brooke thought a minute. Then she opened her mouth again.

"The wheels on the bus go 'round and 'round, 'round and 'round . . ."

I leaned over my logbook, chewing hard at the wad of gum in my mouth. The words *going the wrong way* stared back at me.

Going the wrong way. I looked out the window. The Illinois Tollway kept whizzing by, like it had for the last hour, taking us farther and farther from Evanston and on toward Wisconsin and the old red brick monster of a schoolhouse that Dad thought he could remodel into a house.

Mom and Dad love old things. We're used to Mom hauling old butter churns and Edison phonographs and stereoscopes home from flea markets and auctions. But filling a house with antiques isn't the same

4

thing as moving into one. I'd only seen pictures of the schoolhouse so far. But that was enough.

Dad should have stuck with his math teaching job at Northwestern University and never even taken this new job in Madison. Then we'd still have our cozy old two-story house in Evanston, two blocks from the Little League field, just down the street from Brent and Toby, and biking distance from the beach. This summer *would* have been the best ever. We all just got ten-speeds. . . . I chomped harder on my gum and shut my logbook.

"Dad, you're going too slow!" Josh stopped bleeping his game and stared out the window. "All the semis are passing us! Come on, Dad! Put the pedal to the metal! Burn rubber!"

The semis *were* passing us. And the other cars. Probably even a little old lady on a moped could get by us.

Dad glanced toward the back seat. "Best mileage at fifty-five," he said calmly, like he always does when we yell at him to speed up. "It saves energy. Safer, too."

It didn't really matter today. When you're going the wrong way, you might as well take your time. I nudged Josh.

"Why are you in such a hurry to get there?" I muttered.

He shrugged. "Anything's better than being squished

5

in this car and listening to Babble Brooke." He started pushing buttons again. "I'm setting it for 'pro' this game. I bet I can beat your best score."

Bleep-bleep-bleep. He didn't care. He really didn't care. And Carrie even *wanted* to move to Wisconsin. Because Dad promised her that she could have her own room when the schoolhouse was finished. And because Caddie Woodlawn used to live in Wisconsin. That made it okay.

"The wheels on the bus go 'round and 'round," sang Brooke loudly. "The wheels on the—" She stopped. "Are we almost there?"

"We still have a way to go," Mom said in a tired voice.

Dad turned up the volume on the radio. A piano concerto blared out from the rear speaker.

"I want to sit down. And there isn't any room." Brooke squeezed backward between Josh and me. "Move over, Josh."

A whole bunch of beeps went off at the same time.

"You're sitting on my game!" Josh yelled. "Get your butt off my star fleet!" He pushed Brooke into Carrie's lap.

"Get off *Caddie Woodlawn!* You're bending the pages!"

"Miss Icicle and me don't have any place to sit!" Brooke was crying now.

"Miss Icicle's *pretend*. She doesn't need any place to sit!" said Carrie.

The back of Dad's neck was very red. He was holding the steering wheel tightly with both hands. Mom looked over at him, then turned around and grabbed Brooke under her armpits.

"I think you and Miss Icicle better sit up front with me," she said. "But be careful of the bleeding heart bush."

The bleeding heart bush was the reason Brooke had spent most of the ride in the back seat instead of on Mom's lap. We gave the bush to Mom on her birthday last year. When we sold the house in Evanston, Mom made the real estate agent write into the contract that the bush was moving with us. So it was sitting in a big, white pail on the floor, by Mom's feet.

"Wisconsin!" Carrie cried, pointing to the big, green road sign. *"Thank you for using the Illinois Tollway.* We're out of Illinois! We're in Wisconsin!"

I picked up my logbook and wrote:

> *Entering new stellar zone. Expect hostile conditions. Possible aliens.*

Then in a tiny scrawl:
> *Beam me back to Evanston, Captain.*

A few minutes later, Carrie leaned forward with a frown. "It doesn't look right."

"What?"

"Wisconsin. It doesn't look right. When we went camping, it was like a forest. And there was forest

7

around Caddie's house, too. This looks just like Illinois."

"Carrie," Mom said patiently, "we camped in the north woods. The whole state isn't like that. It's rolling hills. Corn country."

"But Caddie Woodlawn—"

"Caddie Woodlawn lived a long time ago! Things were a lot different then."

"But Dad said we'd be like pioneers! And I thought . . . I thought . . ." Her voice faded away. I looked sideways at her.

"Don't be dumb," I said. "Wisconsin isn't still full of log cabins, you know."

"Shut up," she hissed. I felt better. Now at least somebody felt as miserable as me.

But Dad got cheerier and cheerier the farther we drove into Wisconsin. "Won't be long now," he said into the rearview mirror as we rolled down the almost empty interstate.

"Does the schoolhouse still look like the pictures you showed us?" Josh asked.

"Pretty much. Your Uncle Doug and I hauled away tons of debris over spring break, including about two inches of pigeon manure covering the floor inside." He grinned at Mom. "And I got the old coal furnace taken apart and hauled away. It was a monster. Took up the whole basement, practically." His voice always sounded peppy when he talked about the schoolhouse.

8

"We *will* be like pioneers, Carrie. We'll pitch both tents, the pup tent and the nine-by-nine. I already have a picnic table in the yard. . . ." Dad's voice went on and on. "Summer adventure . . . I know it's an adjustment . . . you'll love it, once it's all fixed up. . . ." And we speeded closer and closer. Off the interstate, down country roads lined with baby cornstalks. "Almost there." He even started whistling in time with Mozart on the radio.

"No trees," Carrie said sadly. "It's so *civilized*."

"Don't be dumb," I said. "Cornfields aren't civilized." I scribbled in my logbook:

> *We are headed where no eleven-year-old*
> *boy has gone before.*

I thought about that a minute. It *had* been a school, after all. I crossed out the entry and wrote:

> *Where no eleven-year-old boy has*
> *lived before.*

"Look!" Josh squeezed next to me to see better out the window. "An accident!"

"Where, where?" Carrie crowded near the window, too. Brooke's legs flew back into the air. She landed headfirst in my logbook.

"I want to see the accident!"

"Get off!" I yelled. "I'm getting smushed! *Off!*"

"A real crash-up!" Josh cried. "There's a car with

its back end all banged up, and something *big* in the ditch. And an ambulance and a police car."

"What happened?" Carrie's voice was low, solemn.

"Whatever it was, they don't need us gawking at it." And Dad swung the Chevette around the whole scene. He actually sped down the road. But Josh kept watching out the back window.

"They're carrying someone out on a stretcher," he reported in the same excited voice. "There's blood—"

"Don't be gory," Mom snapped. "Get away from the back window. Settle down, children!"

We sped past the accident. Then, about ten minutes later, Dad pulled the car onto a weedy lot surrounded by cornfields.

"Here we are!" His outstretched arms swept over the whole place: the weeds, the dirt driveway that led nowhere, the heap of junk toward the back, the tilled garden plot on the other side, and the big, red brick building standing right smack in the middle of the weeds.

"That's . . . our new house?" Josh said in a small voice.

We all stared. And we forgot about the accident.

2

"Are we camping in our new house?" Brooke asked. "Is there a lake? And woods?"

"No lake," I muttered and gave a mighty whack on the tent stake.

"No woods," Carrie said, holding her tent stake and staring sadly off into space.

"Just cornfields." Josh hooked a big rubber band to his tent stake and pulled it back like a slingshot.

Cornfields to the north. Cornfields to the south. Cornfields across the street. And a big, weedy lot under our feet.

And in the middle of the weeds, to the right of the tents—the disaster. The red brick disaster, with its new black roof, and its boarded windows, and its big hole of an inside, all full of cobwebs and old boards and dirt, and probably bats and rats. And its faded sign: *Consolidated School District*. It wouldn't take a carpenter to turn it into a home. It would take the Wizard of Oz.

"Plenty of room for the kids to play. Good, clean, fresh air. Land around us instead of subdivisions." Dad spread his arms out toward the garden. "And look, Lynn, the seeds that Doug planted for me a few weeks ago are poking through. The peas are up front, and the tomatoes and cucumbers are at this end. And there's the tripod for the pole beans."

When Dad was born, someone up in heaven must have waved a corncob over him and programed his brain with vegetables. Back in Evanston, he always spent half the summer fussing over his garden. And this new garden was three times as big as the old one. That was probably why the old run-down schoolhouse didn't bother him. In the summer, Dad didn't need a house. He'd just as soon pull up a cauliflower for a pillow and sleep outside.

"Mmm . . ." Mom's face looked like it usually does right before a big trip, when she's scribbling a dozen lists on the kitchen table. The bigger the job, the more lists she makes. I could just imagine the lists going through her head right now. This place needed *every-thing*. Of course, she saw the schoolhouse over spring break. But then we weren't moving *in*.

"Well," she said in a loud, forced voice, "we've certainly got our work cut out for us this summer. Right, kids?"

"Got the tents ready?" Dad walked toward us. He'd

12

taken off his shirt. The letters *Northwestern U* stared at me from his T-shirt. "Mom and the girls and I will take the big tent. Ryan, you and Josh get the pup tent."

"Good. Now we won't have to listen to Babble Brooke all night," Josh said.

Brooke talked in her sleep. Sometimes in the middle of the night, she'd wake everyone up in the house with her hollering. The kid never shut up.

"This tent business is just for the first few weeks, anyway," Dad went on. "Uncle Doug will be driving from Edgerton a few days a week to help and to bring us water. We'll get the place livable in no time at all." He stood with his arms folded across his chest, staring at the schoolhouse. "The new roof looks good, doesn't it?"

"Terrific," I muttered. Dad gave me a long look. He put his hands in his pockets.

"It's going to be a clear night," he said. "You should get out your binoculars, Ryan. It's a lot clearer for stargazing out here in the country. And speaking of binoculars"—he lowered his voice—"look." He pointed up into the tree. "There's a scarlet tanager up on the third branch."

Josh pointed at Brooke, who was walking over with her load of branches. "Here comes a two-legged warty-bird," he said.

"We need firewood when we camp," Brooke called out. "Did we bring marshmallows?"

13

"Brooke," I began, "this isn't like the other times we camped—" But she was already skipping away.

Five minutes later, she was back. "Where's the bathroom place?" she yelled. "I can't find it and I hafta go."

"The outhouse. Over there," Carrie pointed.

Brooke skipped toward it.

"Hey!" she cried. "It's just like a trash can! It even has a lid!"

Dad shook his head and grinned. "The outhouse is temporary, too. Just until I can get the plumbing put in. The old septic system is still functional."

"I'm Oscar the Grouch, sitting on my trash can!" Brooke's high-pitched voice floated over the outhouse roof.

Josh grinned. "That's a good name for the john— Oscar's Place."

An outhouse. A weed field. Satellites were circling all around the earth; the Trekkers were having a sci-fi convention in Chicago, and here we were—pioneers in a cornfield, with a seventy-five-year-old schoolhouse that had a black hole for an inside.

I picked up an old piece of board lying beside the schoolhouse and grabbed Brooke's crayon box from the back seat of the car. Josh named the john; I could christen the schoolhouse.

The black crayon was only about an inch long, but there was enough left for me to write *THE BLACK HOLE* in big capitals across the board. I picked up my hammer and an old nail lying in the dirt. I hung my sign right over the splintery door. It was a better sign than *Consolidated School District*.

Dinner was hot dogs. And we did have a campfire over a little ring of stones in the corner of the yard. That made Brooke even more confused.

"Do we drive somewhere to rent a boat?" she asked, looking out over the cornfields with a little, puzzled frown.

Josh started to giggle. So did Carrie.

"Well," I said, trying to straighten out the corners of my mouth, "you never can tell. It might come in handy. Every schoolhouse should have a boat."

"It might flood," Josh said solemnly.

"And we'd be stuck out here," said Carrie. "We'd have to sit on the roof till the helicopter came."

"Row, row, row your boat," sang Josh, "over the rows of . . . um . . . corn. Merrily, merrily, merrily, merrily. Life is . . ." he paused, thinking. "Uh . . ."

"Yeah, smarty?" I challenged. "Life is what?"

"Life is when you're born!" yelled Brooke. Everyone clapped. She bowed, holding out her hot dog like a microphone.

"Nah nah na-na-na," she twanged, swinging her rear end around. "Nah na—"

Josh jumped up, too. "No, no, not that one!" He waved his hot dog stick in the air. I waved mine back. And then we were all jumping around, fencing with our sticks, running through the weeds.

15

"Settle down!" Dad shouted. "Settle down before one of you gets hurt. Those sticks have been in the fire, remember?"

But we just kept running and yelling, like wackos. Well, after all, we'd just found out we were going to spend the rest of our growing-up days in the middle of a cornfield.

Mom finally caught Brooke by her jeans as she ran by, and scooped her up.

"Come on, Loretta Lynn, time for bed."

From across the yard came an indignant howl: "Mom, look what you did! You got Miss Icicle's pigtail stuck in the tent zipper!"

3

I rested my elbows carefully on my knees and aimed the binoculars up at the sky. I'd never admit it to Dad, but there was one good thing about this place after all. The night sky. Tonight the stars were almost as bright and thick as the star shows at the Adler Planetarium in Chicago.

I focused on the handle of the Big Dipper. Mizar, the second star in the handle, has a companion star, Alcor. I never could find it back in Evanston. But here it was almost as easy to spot as the others. And there were Cassiopeia and Scorpius. At least that part of the neighborhood hadn't changed much.

"Hey, let me use the binoculars." Josh was a big, dark lump beside me all of a sudden. "You've had them ever since it got dark. They're not just yours, you know."

"You don't need binoculars to find the moon," I

17

said. "And that's the only thing you'd recognize up there."

"Very funny. Come on. It's my turn."

"You wouldn't even want them if I wasn't using them!"

The binoculars should be mine. I'm the one who's going to be an astronomer or an astronaut someday. I'm the one who stuck star posters all over my bedroom walls—when I still had bedroom walls. I'm the one who joined the Junior Trekkers and got the Captain Kirk Logbook.

"Give me a *turn*!"

"Boys!" Mom's voice called out from the big tent. "It's getting late. And we've got a lot to do tomorrow."

I pulled the binoculars' strap off my head and plopped it onto Josh's. "Here. Now, you're supposed to look through this end—"

A sideways kick pushed me into the weeds. I started to get up. Then I stopped—and stared.

There was a light out on Highway 12. Soft, glowing, rectangle-shaped—and coming our way.

My stomach felt like it got hit with a Frisbee at full speed.

"Holy cow," Josh croaked. "What *is* it?"

I licked my lips. That was about all I could do. If someone had leveled a stunner at me, I couldn't have felt more frozen.

"It's a . . . it's a . . . I think it's a UFO," I gulped. All

18

these years of watching space movies and reading space books, and it was finally happening. To me.

"Down!" Josh grabbed my arm. "It's coming!"

We both hit the ground. It was very close now, still glowing like a fluorescent light, still moving silently, smoothly, like a Hovercraft.

Weeds prickled my arms and neck. Some kind of bug was crawling in my sock. But I didn't move. I didn't hardly breathe. Just lay there, watching that blob of light roll toward our lot. Long, wavery, glowing. I stared so hard, my eyeballs hurt.

And then, as suddenly as it had appeared, it faded back, rolling in the other direction, toward the dark cornfields.

I couldn't swallow. My throat was very dry. My forehead was sweaty. My heart was going crazy.

We stared at each other. Josh's eyes were two huge circles in the night. He was breathing fast. Old matter-of-fact Josh, who always acts so brave and who giggles at the scary parts in the horror movies. He wasn't giggling now.

"Ryan . . . what—"

"Like I said, it's a . . . a . . . UFO." I could hardly get the words out. Unbelievable. Here on a skinny country road, surrounded by cornfields.

"But—"

"Don't tell anyone, okay?" I whispered. My voice was shaky.

"Yeah, but Ryan," his fingers were practically pinching the skin off my arm, "are UFOs supposed to look like . . . busses?"

"Maybe we didn't see it in the first place," Josh said for the third time. He threw the dish towel over his shoulder and started setting dominoes on top of the just-dried cereal bowls. "Maybe we just imagined it."

"Shh," I hissed. "Do you want the whole world to know?" I wasn't worried about Mom and Dad. They were ripping up the warped floor inside the schoolhouse, with Rachmaninoff on the radio to keep them company. But Carrie was just a few yards away, sweeping out the big tent. "It's just between *us*."

I sloshed the cereal bowl in the soapy-water dishpan, then in the rinse-water pan. "We didn't imagine it. How could we both imagine a spaceship that looked like a bus, for pete's sake?" I wrung out the dishrag. "There. Done with the last stupid bowl." Back in Evanston, we had a dishwasher. "Now let's go somewhere and talk." I started to dump out the dishwater.

"Wait. Don't dump it. I need it." Josh set more dominoes in a line by the bowls, then put one of Brooke's play-family people on the highest piece of the staircase, right over the dishpan. He grinned at me.

"Think I can make her fall in the dishpan?"

"Would you get serious for once! I don't *care* if she falls in the water. I'm talking about our UFO."

"It was shaped like a bus."

"So who says UFOs have to look like flying saucers?"

He didn't answer. Instead, he gave the first domino a little push. It knocked into the next one, and the whole row bent sideways, pushing at the staircase.

"Too high. It won't fall over," I said smugly.

"Yes, it will."

The last domino wobbled there a second, leaning against the staircase. Josh jiggled the table. The diving board tilted. Brooke's little girl went flying and fell in the dishpan with a splash.

"You cheated."

Josh picked her up. Then he looked at me. His face didn't have that proud, smug look it usually did when his setups worked. He looked very serious.

"I've been thinking. About that bus thing. It reminded me of something. . . ." He turned the little girl figure over and over in his hand. Then he looked back up at me. There was a weird look on his face. Scared almost.

"Ryan, remember that accident we saw when we drove here?"

"What's that got to do with anything?"

"Well," he said slowly, "I got a good look at the whole thing out the back window when Dad drove away. And . . . I saw what was lying in the ditch, all banged up."

"What?" His voice and the look on his face were giving me a creepy feeling.

21

"It was a bus." His voice was low, solemn. "Same kind, except for the light."

I stared back at him.

"You mean . . ." I licked my lips, "you mean, what we saw . . . isn't like a . . . UFO? You mean it's like a . . ." I could hardly say it. "Like a . . . ghost?"

He nodded.

Just then Brooke came running across the yard. "I found a new friend," she called out, all smiles. "His name's Norbert. He's real old. He lives on the other side of the cornfield. He's going to visit us sometime!"

Josh and I just kept staring at each other. The goose-bumpy feeling was zapping me hard.

"Maybe it'll come back," I said slowly. "We'll find out. We'll keep watch. You and me."

4

Captain's Log: Stardate June 19, Friday:

Landing crew has set up base on alien planet (from here on called Planet Cornfield, since cornfields are the main form of life).

Sighted possible alien craft Monday. Kept guard posted (Josh and me) every night since. But nothing's happened yet.

Planet Cornfield is bo-ring. No Little League. No Lake Michigan to swim in. No TV. No friends. Just floors that need ripped and water that needs carried and gardens that need weeded.

The Black Hole looks about the same. First thing Mom wants is a toilet. The well drillers come next week.

P.S. Dad's growing a beard.

Map of Planet Cornfield

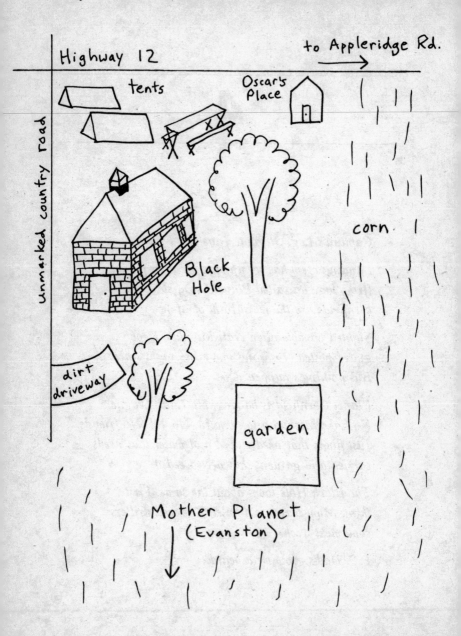

Highway 12

to Appleridge Rd.

tents

Oscar's Place

Unmarked country road

Black Hole

corn

dirt driveway

garden

Mother Planet (Evanston)

"We just imagined it, and we'll never see it again, and I've got fifty-two mosquito bites from sitting out every night," Josh said. He poured a cup of water on his head and down his neck. He sighed. "Not quite the same as Lake Michigan, but at least it's cold."

"We *have* to keep on watching. Look, it's only been a week. Don't give up so fast. Anyway,"—I changed my tactics—"it'll probably be too hot to sleep in the tent."

Josh poured the rest of the water over his head, turning his curly hair into dark, wet ringlets on his forehead. "I know," he sighed again. "Must be ninety degrees out here. I wish there was lemonade in the cooler. Or ice cream. I wish—"

"Carrie Evans—that is a cucumber patch, not a gymnastics mat," Dad called out in a slow, even voice. "Go turn cartwheels somewhere else." He pulled his T-shirt off, wiped his forehead with it, and tossed it out of the garden. "It's too hot for acrobatics, anyway. Too hot for digging, too." But he bent back over his shovel.

"There's nothing else *to* do!" Carrie cried. "I finished my chores, and I've read all my books, and I know *Caddie* almost by heart, and there's no TV. There's nothing to do!"

"Try judo," Josh called out. He tossed his cup and leaped up, feet spread apart, and landed with his arms in a judo pose. *"Hi-yah!"*

Suddenly, a bloodcurdling screech sounded from the tent. Then Brooke burst out, running like she was

25

being chased by bloodhounds. Howling like she *was* a bloodhound.

"You're a terrible, awful Mommy, and I'm never ever going to let you put that awful medicine on my wart again! You burned me! I'm burnt!" She tore across the yard, screaming.

"What a big, brave girl," Mom called loudly, trying to catch up with her. "It'll only sting for a little while, Brooke, honey." She wiped her forehead. "Come on, Brooke. Sit down here like a good girl. It's too hot to run around. Let's have supper."

"Any nice cold things?" Carrie asked hopefully.

Mom shook her head. "I'm afraid it's potluck today, kids. I'm going for groceries tomorrow. Let's see, there's leftover stew, two hard-boiled eggs, some cheese and celery. . . ."

"Stew! On a day like this?" Carrie groaned. Then her voice changed. "Hey, there's the mailman! Maybe I finally got a letter from Rachel." She tore across the yard, then came back a few seconds later and tossed an envelope at me.

"For Ryan. *I* had friends in Evanston, too. Why doesn't anybody write *me!*"

The letter was from Brent.

Dear Ryan,

The Cardinals have lost three practice games so far. I'm catcher. Toby's shortstop.

26

We've been swimming at the beach.
 How's Wisconsin?
 Your friend,
 Brent

"What's it say?" Josh tried to read over my shoulder. I shoved him back angrily.

"Read your own letters, nosy!" I stuffed the letter in my pocket. *I* was supposed to be shortstop. If I'd been there, maybe they wouldn't have lost all three games.

I stared around the table. Josh and Carrie had already grabbed the hard-boiled eggs. Mom was spreading peanut butter on the last nonheel for Brooke. All that was left was stew and heels and cheese.

"This is a lousy supper," I muttered.

"That's enough," Dad said, pointing his mustard knife at me. His new beard gave his face a real stern look when he glared.

"Brent and Toby are probably swimming in Lake Michigan right now."

"Ryan—"

"I want to go swimming," Brooke whimpered. "Water would make my wart feel better."

Dad crunched down on a celery stick. "Brooke, honey, we're not as close to the beach as we used to be."

Brooke dropped her sandwich.

"I want to watch *Sesame Street*." Her lip trembled.

27

"I want to see Oscar and Big Bird. I haven't seen them for a long time."

Josh shook his head sadly. "We can't turn the TV on. It's in Evanston."

Brooke's chin wobbled. "I don't want to camp here any more," she said in a small, quivery voice.

"Oh, we wouldn't have time for TV, even if we could watch it," Dad said in a fake hearty voice. "We're busy accomplishing things, instead of rotting our brains in front of the tube. Like the pioneers. Like Caddie Woodlawn." He nodded at Carrie.

"But she had woods. And Indians. And wild animals," Carrie answered mournfully. "All we have is . . . is . . ."

"A black hole," I finished for her.

Dad took a deep breath. "Speaking of black holes," he said in a slow, calm voice that meant he was trying to control his temper, "tonight I'm going to try to install an outlet so we can get more light inside the schoolhouse. There's already electricity to the box. I'll need some help." He stared at us a second. No one said anything.

I stole a look at Josh. Now we'd probably be stuck on ladders holding flashlights and stuff for Dad until midnight. So much for our plan for a nighttime ghost watch. Dad's projects never went right the first time.

Mom set down her glass. "Now listen to me, all of you. Where's that old pioneer spirit? This is going to be our new home. And you'll have just as much fun

28

as you make up your minds to have. Bloom where you are." It was an order. Like she was talking to her bleeding heart bush, instead of her bleeding heart kids.

I stared back at her gloomily. The letter from Brent had made me feel worse than I had since we moved here.

Carrie stared up at the tree overhead and chewed her fingernails. "I suppose I could . . . build a tree house," she said in a resigned voice. "Then maybe I'd feel like I was in the woods at least. Maybe."

"Here, I know what'll cheer you all up. I've got a surprise." Mom opened the small extra cooler and lifted out a flat plastic container. "Aunt Edna sent over a pie with Uncle Doug this morning. Strawberry glaze!" She lifted the lid and set it on the table. "Look!"

Brooke took one look and laid her head down on her arms.

"It doesn't have a roof!" she sobbed. "I can't eat a pie without a roof!"

This was definitely the worst day of the whole summer.

I wished I was five so I could howl, too.

5

The boarded-up schoolhouse was dark enough during the day. At night it was almost spooky. The lanterns and flashlights threw shadows across the piles of supplies and clutter on the floor, turning them into dark, shapeless blobs. Spiders and other crawly things moved about in the black corners. It was a hard light to work in. Dad's mood was getting worse by the minute.

"Out of wire connectors," he muttered, climbing down from the ladder. "I think the hardware store's still open. May as well drive in now so the night's not a total loss." He turned off the symphony playing on the radio on the floor.

"Did I hear you say hardware store?" Mom walked in. "I've got a whole list of things I need. I'll come along too." She turned to us. "You'll be all right while we go into town, won't you? We shouldn't be too long."

"Sure. We're not babies, you know." I nudged Josh and pointed to my watch. Still time for our ghost patrol.

Five minutes later, the Chevette was pulling out of the driveway, and Josh and I were heading for our corner with the binoculars and the flashlight and the mosquito spray.

"Dang mosquito, go suck somebody else's blood." Josh slapped his arm. "If we don't see anything tonight, I quit."

"What are you doing?" a voice whispered loudly from halfway across the yard. It sounded high. We both jumped. I dropped the mosquito spray.

"Are you watching stars? Can I watch, too?"

Carrie. It was only Carrie. I let out a long, slow breath.

"Where are you?"

"In the tree. My board fell down." She sounded forlorn. "All the boards I tried fell down. This is a lousy tree-house tree. And now I can't even see what I'm doing."

"So give up and go to bed." She wasn't supposed to be hanging around. It was our ghost patrol.

"You and Josh got to help Dad. And Brooke's asleep. And Mom and Dad went shopping. *There's nothing to do!*"

"So read *Caddie Woodlawn* again."

A branch fell somewhere near my feet.

"Okay, okay, I was just kidding."

31

"*You* should read *Caddie*. So you'd know how brothers are supposed to act. Her brothers did things with her. They—" she stopped. Her voice dropped to a croaky whisper. "What's—*that?*"

I spun around.

There it was, down the road. The alien bus craft. Glowing, just like before. Gliding closer.

"What . . . is it?" Carrie croaked again. Closer, at ground level. I hadn't even heard her swing down.

I lifted the binoculars. It was hard to focus. My fingers were shaking.

The thing was long. Rectangle-shaped, just like before. Fluorescent. Wheels on the bottom. A window in the front . . .

One head. Two heads. Three heads. The last one . . . had a horn . . . coming out the top.

"Invasion," I mumbled. "Aliens."

"What!" Josh grabbed the binoculars. "Holy cow!" He let go of them and took a step back.

"Let me look!" Carrie grabbed the strap.

"Androids. Body snatchers." I was still mumbling like an idiot. Something inside of me was going *boing*. Even my chewing gum suddenly wouldn't work. It stuck in a big wad in my throat.

The light rolled closer.

"Get down! Get down!" We all dove for the weeds. Just then a loud, high-pitched voice yelled from across the yard.

"Stop it! Stop it right now, Josh, you dummy."

Brooke! She was talking in her sleep again.

"Stop it!" she hollered. Then even louder, "I said *stop!*"

The bus stopped. Right by the mailbox in front of the schoolhouse.

"That dummy Brooke."

"Come on! Back to the tent!"

"We can't. They—it—will see us."

"Not in the dark!"

"Maybe they can see in the dark."

"We can't just stay here and be pulverized or something!"

"I'm not budging!"

The whispers flew back and forth. I had a dozen new mosquito bites. And a bad heart all of a sudden. It was pounding like a bongo drum.

Something grabbed my shirt. Josh. "Th-the door," he gulped. "It's—holy cow."

It was opening. There was something—no, some-one—in the doorway.

No horns. Just a regular head. Long, thick, brown hair. A T-shirt. Jeans. Just a regular—girl. I mean, if you could call someone all wavy and lit up regular.

"She looks like she's my age," Carrie whispered. She was holding my other shirttail.

Josh pulled on his side of the shirt. "Here comes another one!"

A second figure moved into the doorway. I held

my breath. This could be it. The one with horns.

But it was another regular head. A woman's. With short gray hair and glasses down at the end of her nose. She stood beside the girl and stared across our yard.

I pressed closer to the dirt. Those glasses could be laser probes. Or X-ray scanners. They'd find us any second. And then the alien with horns would come out, all green and scaly.

"Who's . . . out there?" The voice was remote, fuzzy, almost like radio static. I could hardly catch the words.

But then another voice called out from the other side of the yard.

"I'm not going to tell you again!" Brooke yelled from the tent. "Shut up!"

The ghost lady's head jerked up. The glasses wavered and flickered on her face. The girl leaned forward, staring into our dark yard.

"Shut up, yourself!" But she sounded more nervous than mad. She turned to the older woman. "Aunt Vira, there's someone hiding out there!"

I felt a little braver. The two people in the doorway were glowing and unsolid, but they weren't exactly horrible monster creatures from outer space. Not with jeans and a T-shirt. Not with a name like Aunt Vira.

"C.C., maybe . . . should . . . back inside." The woman's voice was fuzzier than the girl's. She sounded more nervous, too.

The ghost girl shook her head. "No. I'm going to

find out who it is." She raised her voice. I could hear the next words clearly. "Who's out there?"

Carrie poked me. "Caddie wasn't afraid of things," she whispered in my ear. "So I won't be either." She started to get up.

I couldn't let Caddie Woodlawn show me up. Or Carrie Evans. I got to my feet before she did.

"Here." My voice was embarrassingly squeaky. I cleared my throat. Captain Kirk never would have sounded like that. And he and the other members of the Enterprise crew had to face strange creatures all the time.

Four ghost eyes focused in my direction. There was no going back now.

"Holy cow," Josh gulped. And then we were all standing, taking one step forward, then another and another. . . .

It wasn't really happening. Couldn't be. I was dreaming. Dreaming that we were all marching toward the alien ghost bus, toward the two glow-in-the-dark people. And somewhere inside crouched the horned beast.

Even Captain Kirk would have had a hard time swallowing.

6

"Kids!" the girl cried. She took a few steps toward us. "Aunt Vira, real live kids!" Her glowy, green face looked excited. I stepped back. So did Josh. She looked harmless, but I wasn't taking any chances.

"Don't go! Please!" She moved even closer. "I need to talk to you."

The other ghost glided up beside her.

"First people . . . since . . . accident." Her voice still faded in and out, like a radio station that wasn't in right. "I . . . beginning . . . think we'd . . . never make contact."

The girl just stood there, with a big fluorescent grin on her face. "Kids," she said happily. "Real live kids."

I wished I could say the same to her.

"But, but—who are you?" Carrie whispered, chewing madly on her fingernail. "Wh-where are you from?"

The ghost girl shook her glowing frizzy hair back off her shoulders. "Middlefield," she said.

You just don't expect a strange glowing person to stand there and tell you they're from Middlefield.

"I mean, I used to be from Middlefield." Her voice was coming through louder and clearer now. "I guess now my home is *that*." She pointed to the bus craft with a sigh of pure disgust. "With all those *books*. Ever since the accident."

Josh and I exchanged looks. What was she talking about?

She kept going, like a spring that was unwinding fast and furious.

"I don't even like books." She tossed her frizzy hair back again. "I just came that one afternoon to help with the shelving. That's *all*. It was Aunt Vira's last day before she retired." She shook her head and held out her ghost arms, like a piece of evidence. "Some retirement, all right."

Little prickles slid up and down my neck when she flapped those ghostly, lit-up arms around. My brain felt like a gearshift stuffed with peanut butter.

"You've got to help us!" Her eyes were like cat's eyes staring out from the dark. "Somebody's got to. Or we'll be trapped forever!"

"Trapped—" I cleared my throat and tried again. My voice sure wasn't very dependable tonight. "Where?"

"In the bookmobile!" Her arm flung out toward the bus, while her ghost eyes stared fiercely at us. "Do

37

you know what it's like to be trapped in one of those things for a whole week? It's like being a hamster in a cage, except there's no exercise wheel."

"A bookmobile," Josh muttered. His first words since "holy cow." He stared from the bus to the girl and back again. "A ghost bookmobile." He nudged me with his elbow. "A ghost bookmobile," he said again in this funny, dazed voice.

Aunt Vira's voice crackled through again. A little louder and clearer this time. ". . . my fault. I was warned. Bad travel day for Scorpios. Both of us . . . Scorpios." She shook her head sadly. "Last day . . . before retirement." Her voice sounded louder with each sentence. Her next words almost came through in one piece: "Ours is not to reason why!"

The girl clapped her hands over her ears. "No more quotes!" She stamped her foot. "We have real live people to talk to now. And they can help us." Her cat's eyes gleamed at us again. "Can't you?"

For once I was glad that the schoolhouse was in the middle of nowhere, and that only the cornstalks could see the strangely glowing bus parked at the roadside and the two glowing ghost people standing in the yard.

Aunt Vira drew herself up proudly and pulled a wavery paperback out of her suit pocket. She held it in front of the girl. "C.C., while . . . trapped here, the only learning we can do is . . . books. And Bartlett's is packed with . . . wisdom of the ages. So mind your tongue!"

"Ages." C.C. rolled her eyes. "Ages and ages and ages. That's how long it's been. Boy, those county people weren't kidding when they said the bookmobile was getting old and might break down. Some breakdown!" She plopped down on the ground, knees crossed, and cupped her chin in her hands. "Trapped," she said again, with a long, dramatic sigh.

"But how can we help?" Carrie's whisper was hushed, respectful. I looked at her quickly. Even in the dark, I recognized that dreamy look on her face. Carrie was actually enjoying the ghosts! Probably the word *bookmobile* did it. Any bus that carried a whole library of books would be okay with Carrie, whether or not it was a ghost.

"Is your motor busted?" Josh's voice wasn't dreamy at all. More like freaked-out. "Is that why you're trapped?"

Aunt Vira's sigh came all the way from her old-fashioned shoes. "Nothing like that. It's called haunting." It wasn't hard to hear her now. The crackling static sound was almost gone. "Most ghosts do get trapped in haunt patterns. Remember Marley in 'A Christmas Carol'? And then there was Hamlet's father. And—"

"But those ghosts got to haunt romantic old English castles or Roman ruins," C.C. cut in. "And we get stuck in a bookmobile in the middle of cornfields."

"But—if you have the bus, why can't you just drive away?" My brain was getting used to the fact that there were two ghosts in the yard. It was starting to move again. "You could drive wherever you wanted to."

"We can't. Because of the accident," Aunt Vira replied patiently. She stared out at the dark stretch of road that was Highway 12. "The bus can't go beyond the point of the accident. It's our barrier."

"Can't you turn around and go in the other direction?"

"Only as far as Highway MM, where the route started," Aunt Vira said. "We're trapped in the bookmobile route on this country road. We can't break free."

"We keep trying," C.C. said sadly. "We get in gear, we zoom down the road, we reach the corner where the accident happened—and that's as far as we get. Every Monday. The other days of the week are even *worse.*" She sighed. "Trapped in the ghostly nothingness. Can't even get through to the real world. All we've got is Monday—same old bookmobile route, same old jinxed intersection and back."

"But—why don't you just leave the bus at the intersection and walk?" Carrie asked with the same dumb, wide-eyed look on her face.

C.C. turned to Aunt Vira. "How do you explain to *mortals?*" She threw out her arms. "In the first place, we need the bus to get to all the places we want to visit." She grinned. "Aunt Vira always wanted to travel when she retired. We have big plans. And in the second place, we can't go very far from the bus, anyway.

It pulls on us. Sort of like . . ." She chewed her glowy lips, thinking hard. "Sort of like . . . gravity. Yeah, that's it. Psychic gravity." She nodded, pleased with herself. "We all had the accident together and it looks like we're gonna be stuck together forever after. Me and Aunt Vira and Peg."

"Peg?" My ears perked up. I looked over at the bookmobile. There was someone or something in there. Those horns.

"Pegasine, really," C.C. said. "Feminine for Pegasus. For our flying unicorn."

"Huh?"

"Aunt Vira's a nut about unicorns," C.C. explained. "So she made one out of this shiny material and stuffed it and hung it from the bus ceiling. That's how the bus got its name. After Pegasine."

The horn in the window. Not invaders. Not body snatchers. A stuffed unicorn.

"But isn't there any way you can break loose?" Carrie asked in the same respectful voice.

C.C. tossed her frizzy hair again. "There sure better be a way. I mean, who wants to be stuck here for the rest of their death?"

Now *that* I could understand. "I know just what you mean," I muttered.

Out of the corner of my eye, I could see Josh moving closer to the bus, reaching out a hand, then pulling it back quickly. If he had his calculator with him, he'd probably be computing how solid it was, or figuring

41

out the magnetic ghost fields. The glowy light of the bus made him look sort of like Dracula.

"We shall find a way," Aunt Vira said firmly, staring off into the darkness. "We must. Then we shall be free to travel anywhere—"

"Las Vegas," C.C. cut in excitedly. "Hollywood, Disney World, New York!"

Aunt Vira peered at her over her glasses. "I was thinking more along the lines of places of history and culture and literature, my dear. Like Europe's medieval castles, or the pyramids, or our own country's historical landmarks. All the wonderful places those books have told us about!" She flung her arm toward the bookmobile. "Yes, we *shall* find a way. There are more powers in heaven and on earth—"

C.C. groaned. "Not another quote!" But Josh cut her off with a little cry.

"Car lights! Mom and Dad are coming!"

Fast as lightning, C.C. and Aunt Vira sped toward the bus. "We'll be back!" C.C. called from the doorway as Aunt Vira started guiding the bus back down the road. "On Monday. We *need* you." Her voice was getting faraway, fuzzy again. "You've got to help us!"

Carrie and Josh and I stood there, watching them disappear down Highway 12, going east, just as Mom and Dad's car rolled in from the south. Then the car lights flooded the yard and we all ran for our tents.

7

I felt very strange the next morning. I tried to act calm and ordinary at breakfast, as if nothing unusual had happened during the night. But Josh must have felt strange, too. And he was no help at all. Just one look at that silly telltale grin stretched over his face, and anyone would have been suspicious.

But, luckily, Dad was too busy staring around the yard to notice Josh's face.

"Beautiful morning. Beautiful morning," he said in a deep, booming voice. "Just think of what all those people eating breakfast inside are missing!" He stretched out his arms toward the yard, the schoolhouse, the whole cornfield planet. With his new beard and tan, he really looked like an outdoorsman.

It wasn't a bad morning. Blue sky, sunny. Even the Black Hole looked a bit more respectable with the weeds mowed down to look like grass.

"Bee-u-tiful morning," Josh echoed. His silly smile stretched even bigger. He arched his eyebrows at me across the table. "Bee-u-tiful," he said again.

I leaned over my bowl quickly, before my face could break into the same silly smirk. Beside me, Carrie madly shoveled in her cereal. One giggle and we'd all be goners. I kicked Josh under the table.

"This old place is really going to look like something when we're finished," Dad went on in the same cheery voice. "The north windows will be delivered in a few days—" He turned to us then. "I bet none of you know why there were so many windows on the north side of the building," he challenged.

"Uh, to waste energy?" Josh asked with a giggle.

"Very funny, smart aleck. I'll tell you why. It's because there wasn't any electricity inside when the place was first built, around the turn of the century. So the pupils got the best writing and reading light from the north side, without any glare from the sun. Now what's so funny about that?" he asked, finally noticing Josh's face.

"N-nothing," Josh giggled.

I grabbed the nearest thing, the bread, and shoved it at him. "Here, eat something," I said, fixing him with my meanest glare. Some secret agent he'd make.

Josh stared at the wrapper. "One hundred percent whole wheat. Wrong kind, like always." His tone was mournful, but he was still fighting a grin.

44

"What's wrong with it?" Brooke held up her piece of bread and stared at it. Big drops of honey slid over the edge.

"Just wait till you get to school and trade sandwiches and find out what good bread tastes like."

Mom pointed her finger at Josh. "Joshua Walden Evans, I'll thank you to quit trying to brainwash your little sister. She's perfectly happy with wholesome bread. That white foam-rubber stuff you kids like so much has absolutely no fiber at all. You might as well eat your pillow."

"My pillow isn't fortified with eight essential vitamins," Josh answered promptly. He giggled again. "Hey, if I was a ghost, I wouldn't need any fiber, would I?"

Carrie and I both choked on our cereal. But Dad grinned back at Josh.

"Then you'd be a whole-white ghost," he shot back.

I didn't like the way the conversation was going at all. I nodded at Carrie and stood up, yanking Josh with me. "Come on. Let's—weed." Anything to get the idiot away.

Dad looked surprised. "Try not to step on the new strawberry plants," he called after us. "And don't pull around the onions, you might disturb the bulbs . . ." Instructions and advice followed us all the way to the garden. Down on our hands and knees, I let Josh have it.

45

"Idiot! Bumble brain! Some spy! Some secret-keeper! You just about gave the whole thing away. Don't you know what poker face means?"

"I didn't give anything away," Josh answered calmly. "They didn't suspect a thing." He squatted beside the green onions and starting tying the tops together with square knots. Across the yard, the well drillers rolled in the driveway and started setting up equipment. "They wouldn't have even believed it if I *had* told them," he ended loudly, over the noise.

"When I first woke up this morning, I didn't even believe it happened," Carrie said. "I thought I'd dreamed it all." She sat back and clasped her arms around her knees. "Imagine—*ghosts*. Real honest-to-goodness ghosts. And they need *our* help. So they can go to all those faraway places Aunt Vira talked about."

"Well, she's a librarian, after all," Josh said matter-of-factly. "A librarian ghost should haunt book places, right?"

"I'm with C.C." I said. "Las Vegas, Disney World."

Carrie pulled out a weed clump and threw it backward over her head. "But what I still don't get is— why can't they just go haunt wherever they want? Why are they stuck here?"

"That always happens to ghosts," I explained. "They get stuck in a place and just keep haunting it. It's usually a place where something awful happened, like a murder. Or like the accident." I felt very smart.

"But why Monday?" Josh yelled over the drilling.

"What happens to them the rest of the week?"

"Well, ghosts have schedules, you know. Some come out at midnight, some on Halloween, some when the moon is full." I banged another weed clump to loosen the dirt. "C.C. and Aunt Vira are Monday ghosts. Because of their bookmobile schedule, I guess."

"But what about the rest of the week?"

"Remember what C.C. said." I made my voice low and spooky. "The rest of the week they're in the 'ghostly nothingness.' "

"But what's a ghostly nothingness?" Josh persisted.

"Some ghost place. I don't know."

"They probably sleep in the bookmobile, like a portable graveyard," Carrie said thoughtfully. She sat back, squishing a tomato plant. "Hey, do you suppose a nonghost can read a book from a ghost bookmobile? I really need a book."

"How are we ever going to be able to help them?" Josh asked. "What can we do?"

"We can climb up into the bus and drive it away for them," I said. "*Three kids and two ghosts escape from Black Hole in bus!* Wouldn't that make a great headline!"

"What in heaven's name . . ." Mom suddenly stood in front of us, one hand on her hip, the other holding the watering can. She stared at the row of knotted onion tops and the squashed tomato plant. "You're supposed to be weeding, not practicing your overhand pitch." She glared at Carrie. "Get off that tomato

47

plant, young lady. You kids better get this mess cleaned up, or your dad's going to *kill* you. Untie those onions, Josh, for goodness' sake. Oh, and look at my poor bush!"

She leaned over her bleeding heart bush, checking the leaves the way she checks Brooke's ears to see if they're clean. "I'll be so glad when we don't have to carry water."

"I know what'll help your plant, Mom," Carrie said in her most helpful voice. "My science teacher last year said that music helps plants grow. He said if you sing to plants, they grow quicker."

"And here comes just the person we need," Josh said. "Hey, Brooke," he hollered. "Do you know any good plant songs? Mom's plant needs a good song so it'll grow."

She ran toward us, her curly pigtails bobbing. "I know a good one! About lettuce."

"Go to it." I waved my arm toward the bush.

Brooke bent over the plant. "O come, lettuce adore him," she hollered out. "O come, lettuce adore him. O come, lettuce adore hi-im, Chri . . . ist the Lord!"

8

Captain's Log: Stardate June 28, Sunday:

The corn is getting very tall. Probably we will all be strangled in our sleep by alien creeping cornstalks.

Brought more stuff from Evanston in U-Haul, including bikes.

There's a park in town, with a swimming pool! Only a few miles away. We can bike there. But not tomorrow.

Tomorrow's MONDAY.

I stretched my bubble gum into a flat, rubbery sheet against my tongue and threw the softball against the schoolhouse wall for the fiftieth time. The nervous waiting feeling was worse than on Christmas Eve. At least Santa Claus was predictable. But who knew *when* the ghost bus would roll down the road, or even if it would really come—or who would be around to see it?

"Let's see, I'll get more groceries today, and do laundry at Doug and Edna's tomorrow, and price joists while I'm in town. . . ." Mom was working on a new list at the picnic table, with her sleeves rolled up and her hair pulled back in a ponytail. "That ought to do it." She held up the list in a good-bye wave as she headed for the car.

"If you're going to town, get me some books, please. Like *Trixie Belden,*" Carrie called from a backbend position. "I need something to make the day go faster until the . . ." Her voice trailed off. She gave me a guilty, upside-down look.

Brooke's voice filled the sudden silence.

"Hi, everybody. I brought my new friend Norbert over," she yelled, skipping along the driveway beside a tall man in bib overalls. He had bushy gray hair and a deep tan.

"Hello, neighbors," he called out in a cheery voice. He pointed his pipe at the schoolhouse. "So you're fixin' the old place up?"

"We're working at it." Dad strode toward him. "I'm Rob Evans."

Norbert leaned forward a little, as if to hear better.

"Norb Spencer. Glad to meet you." He stared at

the schoolhouse again. "It's a shame the way this place has gone downhill the last few years. Lord, I can remember when it was full of kids: the Peterson kids from the farm by the river, and the Richardses, and then there was our family—"

"You went to this school?" Dad's eyes lit up like a Christmas tree. "Would you like to see what we're doing to the inside? Maybe you could tell me some things about the old furnishings." The history gears were practically turning somersaults in Dad's brain.

Norbert pointed his pipe at my sign tacked over the front door. "*The Black Hole*, huh? Somebody studyin' astronomy around here?"

I was a little embarrassed. "I'm not studying it, really. It's, um, a hobby."

"What's that, son?" he cocked his head toward me.

"I said it's a hobby," I yelled.

He nodded thoughtfully. "My brother Bill lives across town. Since he's been retired, he's got himself a real telescope. He always did like space stuff, even when we were kids. Read a lot of them Buck Rogers comic strips."

Dad pulled the schoolhouse door wide open. "Want to take a look around?" They disappeared inside, just as Mom backed the car out of the driveway.

"You kids stick around now," she called before driving away. "Your dad might need help."

I blew another bubble and grabbed a tree branch to swing from. As if we'd *go* anywhere!

"Help!" yelled Carrie. "I'm stuck!" She was doing a handstand, with her feet propped up against the brick wall. "My feet won't come down! And if I let go with my hands—"

"Hey, what's that funny light coming down the street?" Brooke cut in, staring down the road.

"What!"

I swallowed my bubble gum. Carrie fell on her head. Josh sailed out of his rope swing.

It couldn't be them. Not with Dad and Norbert just inside the door, and Mom barely out of sight down the road.

But it was.

"Come *on!*" Carrie tore across the yard, rubbing at her sore head, with Josh and me close behind.

Brooke just stood there. For the first time in her whole five years, she didn't have anything to say. Not one word. She just stood there and stared.

9

"You're here! You're here!" C.C. burst through the door before it was even open. She just went right through the glowing stuff, took a flying leap, and landed almost on the septic pipe. "Oh, I'm so glad to see you!"

"Wait," I cut in, talking fast and low. "Our dad's right inside the schoolhouse. It's not safe for you to be here. He could come out any second!"

"Oh, dear." Aunt Vira bit her lip. "I knew we should have waited until nighttime to break through." She waved a finger toward C.C. "It's called 'Look before you leap,' my girl. You're always too impatient."

"He who hesitates is lost," C.C. shot back. "I'm getting to know that book as good as you, Aunt Vira. Anyway, I had to get away. Bustrophobia." She tossed her thick, frizzy hair back off her shoulders. She didn't look one bit worried. If Dad came out right now, she'd probably run up and give him a big ghost hug.

"Hey, you gotta go!" I was getting panicky.

"But we have something to tell you!" C.C. cried. She pulled a little pamphlet out of her bag. "Aunt Vira found it, but I'll read it for you."

I looked back at the schoolhouse, then at C.C., then at the bus. I bit my lip. "Okay, but hurry up with it."

C.C. cleared her throat importantly and held the pamphlet way out, like an actor reading a script.

"It's about astrology. Now listen:

> 'Scorpios: You will enjoy a period of unexpected breakthroughs in the coming weeks. A good time to travel.' "

She waved the book at us. "And get *this*:

> 'Scorpios: You will encounter new and special people who will point you in new directions of future achievements.' "

She shut the book. The gauzy pages whooshed instead of banged. She beamed at us. "That's *you*. You're the special people who will point us in new directions. It says so right here in this book. We were meant to meet you!"

"We have to be very careful, you know," Aunt Vira added. "Not just *any* mortal would accept the fact of our ghostliness, much less try to help us."

"Does your book say just how we're going to help?"

54

I began, but just then Brooke got her blabber-tongue back.

"What's your name?" she demanded, staring at C.C., then at Aunt Vira. "And why do you look so silly?"

"C.C.'s my name," C.C. answered. "It stands for cotton candy. I got nicknamed that because I pigged out so much at the fair last year."

"No kidding?" I stared at her. Strange to think of C.C. stuffing in cotton candy. I mean, she almost looked like she was made out of the stuff. And in the bright sunlight, she hardly showed up at all; even the bus seemed less visible, a hazy blob that shimmered in the sunshine—like looking through smoke.

Brooke kept staring. "Is that your costume?" she whispered. "For Halloween?"

"Yep. And for Christmas and Easter. For St. Patrick's Day, I'll paint it green."

"C.C.—" Aunt Vira's voice was worried. "This is no time to crack jokes. We must leave *now*. Next time, we'll come at night."

"Can you come any time you want on Mondays?" Josh asked.

"We're getting better at it," C.C. said proudly.

"You see," Aunt Vira explained, "our ability to get through to the physical world seems to depend on the strength of our concentration. The first time, it was more or less an accident. Now we're getting more experience. We can control the time a bit better."

"What's *your* name?" Brooke turned to Aunt Vira.

Aunt Vira's face softened. Even ghosts are suckers for Brooke's act.

"You can call me Aunt Vira." She patted Brooke's head; Brooke's curls went right through her hand. Then Aunt Vira glanced nervously back at the schoolhouse. "C.C., we've stayed far too long. Get in the bus."

"But we have to tell them your idea about the projection!" C.C. cried. "About psychic powers and teleporting and astral bodies and all. And we don't know their names or their signs."

I was practically hopping up and down in the weeds, I was so nervous. C.C. was as big a blabbermouth as Brooke. If she didn't shut up soon—

But now Carrie was blabbing, too. "I'm Carrie," she said loudly, tossing her braids back. "And I'm a Taurus."

"I'm Brooke." Brooke gave C.C. her sweetest smile. "And I'm an Oreo."

"Scorpio, dummy. Scorpio," said Josh. He scuffed his shoe in the dirt, then looked up at C.C. and Aunt Vira. "And Dad says astrology is a bunch of bull."

"Oh, yeah?" C.C. cried. "Oh, yeah? I suppose your dad doesn't believe in ghosts, either!"

"Uh—he may in a minute," I said, swallowing hard. I nodded my head toward the schoolhouse. The door was opening.

"Well, Norb, it's been good talking to you. You

come on over any time." Dad's voice boomed across the yard.

"They're coming!"

C.C. could move like wind when she wanted to. Before I even got the words out, she was back in the bus.

"Next Monday," she called in a loud whisper. "At night. Midnight. That's the best time to try the projection." The next moment, the bus was a blurry haze moving down the road.

"Like I said, it's a mighty fine thing you folks are doin', fixin' up the old schoolhouse to live in." Norbert's voice was close and loud. "And with all these helpin' hands, you'll have her fit as a fiddle in no time."

"Hey, helping hands," Dad called to us from the doorway. "What's so interesting out there in the street?"

I breathed a long, wobbly sigh of relief. He hadn't seen the bus or the ghosts. This time.

"Uh, nothing," Josh said. He poked me. "What are we going to try at midnight?" he whispered. "What the heck is a projection?"

"I don't know."

"Neither do I," Carrie said. We all stared at each other.

"Hey, Daddy," Brooke squealed, running across the yard. "I just saw a ghost!"

My heart skipped three and a half beats. I looked at Carrie and Josh; they stared back at me, wide-eyed.

But Dad just grinned.

"A ghost, huh?" he said, with a wink at Norbert. "What happened to Miss Icicle?"

"Oh, she melted," Brooke answered cheerfully. She tugged at his shirt. "Daddy, is it almost Halloween? I want to be a ghost, too. And I want a bus for my costume!"

10

"The question is—how are we all going to meet outside at midnight?" Carrie asked. She ripped open a pea pod and ran her thumb down it, pushing peas off into the bowl. "We have to have a plan. That's what the kids in the mystery books do. They don't leave it all up to luck."

"You read too much," I muttered. Ever since Mom got the stack of Trixie Belden books at the library, all Carrie talked about was clues and alibis and hideouts. "The question *is*—what's a projection? We still haven't figured that one out."

"The question *is*—who can shoot a pea all the way to Oscar's Place?" Josh pulled half a plastic straw out of his pocket and set a pea inside. "Watch this," he bragged.

The little pea sailed through the air and pinged against the outhouse wall.

"Anyone for spit pea soup?" Josh bowed. "Now, for my next trick, I'll set up a bunch of dominoes leading toward Oscar's can, then shoot a pea to set them off, see—"

"We're supposed to be filling the bowl, not spitting peas all over the yard!" Carrie cried. "If Mom and Dad see you, they'll probably change their minds about letting us go to the pool this afternoon, and it'll be all your fault!"

"They'll never know," Josh answered calmly. "Dad got mad at the toilet pipes and went jogging. And Mom's out shopping for old school desks, remember?" He shot another pea.

Carrie tried to grab his straw. "You still haven't answered my question! Use your brilliant brain to figure out how I can get out next Monday for C.C. and Aunt Vira. It's easy for you two. You have your own tent. But I don't!"

"Tell Mom you have to get up to go to the bathroom."

"And just what am I supposed to say when I get back an hour later?"

Josh thought a minute. "I know. Tell her you're consecrated."

"What!"

"The word's constipated, dummy." I threw another pea in the air. With a whole afternoon of swimming to look forward to, even a half bushel of peas to shell

60

wasn't so bad. I threw one at Josh. It hit him in the nose.

"All right for you!" He shot one at my forehead. I jumped up, spilling my lapful of pods.

Josh stooped over and spread out his arms in a wrestling stance. We circled a few seconds. He lunged first. I grabbed his leg on the way down, and we both sprawled.

"Two-point takedown!" yelled Norbert's voice from across the yard.

"Uh-oh, Ryan and Josh are fighting!" Brooke cried, running along beside Norbert.

"No, they're not. They're wrestling. There's a difference." Norbert crouched beside us, circling like a referee, watching every move.

"Good roll-away. There's the reversal!" he called as Josh struggled out from under me. We were pretty evenly matched. I'm taller, but we weigh almost the same. We tumbled, grabbed, rolled, broke away, got up, crashed down. Norbert called each move.

"Good job!" he cried, clapping us on the back as we finally broke away, panting.

Brooke swung a metal pail in front of us. "Norbert gave me this. It's to keep my important things in." She bobbed her head up and down.

"It's an old lard pail. We used 'em for lunch boxes when I was a kid." Norbert tweaked Brooke's pigtail.

61

"What did you take in your lunch pail, Norbert?" Brooke asked. "Did you have bologna sandwiches and potato chips?"

"Well, let's see . . . I loved fried egg sandwiches and baked bean sandwiches best, myself. But there were all kinds. Kids that didn't have much money usually just had lard sandwiches or jelly."

"Lard—sandwiches?" Carrie made a face. "You mean like shortening?"

"Yuk," said Josh."Lard. Baked beans. Give me peanut butter any day. And candy bars."

"Oh, we had chocolate. They handed it out in school." Norbert winked as we all stared. "Chocolate-covered iodine tablets."

"What!"

"Iodine! You *ate* iodine?"

"Salt wasn't iodized back then." Norbert looked like he was enjoying our surprise. "People had trouble with goiters. So our teachers gave us iodine tablets at school, the way kids nowadays take vitamins." A big smile stretched across his face. "I remember one time the teacher was out of the room and I practically ate the whole box!"

"What's a goiter?" Brooke tugged at his shirt.

"It's a swelled-up lump by the throat," Norbert answered.

"My goiter's a wart," Brooke said, touching her finger. "We put medicine on it every day. But it's not chocolate."

Norbert looked up, shading his eyes with his hands as a noisy car wheezed down the road. "I'd know the sound of that old Studebaker anywhere. That's my brother Bill coming." He waved his arms at the driver. "Over here."

"So this is where you've been keeping yourself." A short, cheery-faced man climbed out of the car. "I've been by your place already, lookin' for you."

"Come on out and see what these folks are doin' to the old schoolhouse. They're fixin' it up to live in." Norbert sounded as proud as if he'd thought the whole idea up himself.

"Is that so?" Bill glanced around. "Mighty ambitious plan." He nodded solemnly, then gave us all a wink. "And I bet old Norb here has been talkin' your ears off with all his stories."

"He was telling us about how he ate a box of chocolate iodine," Josh volunteered.

"Ah," Bill said. He put his arm around Norbert's shoulder and spoke loudly in his ear. "And did you tell 'em about the time you got your tongue stuck to the water pump in the dead of winter?"

"Now, now, just about every boy in the school tried that trick some time or other," Norbert said. "Wasn't just me." He turned to us. "You know—stickin' your tongue to metal to see if it'll freeze stuck?"

Josh and I exchanged glances. That wasn't such an old-fashioned trick. I'd tried sticking my tongue to a chain link fence just last year.

"But how did you get your tongue unstuck?" Brooke asked, wide-eyed.

Norbert winked at her. "Had to stay there till spring," he said very seriously.

Bill tapped Norbert. "Say, did you hear the talk about a funny floaty light on this road a few nights back?"

My breath caught in my throat. I shot a quick, panicky glance toward Josh and Carrie.

Norbert grinned. "Little green men, too?" he asked in a teasing voice.

"*I* wasn't the one that saw it," Bill shot back. "Some other farmers did. They were talkin' about it down at the tavern. A floaty light. On this very road."

I bit my lip hard and stared straight ahead, not daring to even look at Carrie or Josh.

But Norbert just kept smiling. "My brother Bill here believes in flyin' saucers," he said to us. "Saw his first little green man when he was about your age."

"Now, what I saw back then don't have nothin' to do with—"

"I know what it was!" Brooke piped up. "It was C.C.'s bus. That's a floaty light!"

"What's that, honey?" Norbert leaned closer.

"C.C.," Brooke shouted. "It was C.C.'s bus!"

"Learnin' some of them Spanish words, are you?" he beamed down at her.

Josh giggled.

"Look, Brooke, there's Dad!" I yelled at the top of

my lungs. I grabbed her hand and pulled her away from Norbert. "Dad's back. Go say hi to him, Brooke."

"Yeah. Sing him a song." Josh gave her a helpful shove.

Dad jogged up the driveway, panting. Sweat dripped down his forehead.

"Whew. That felt good. First real exercise I've had in a long time."

"Daddy, Norbert's here—and his brother Bill," Brooke called out.

Dad lifted his hand in a wave. "Be right with you—after I get a drink." He bent over the faucet.

"Watch out, Daddy!" Brooke yelled, running toward him. "Don't touch the metal part with your tongue. It'll stick, and you'll have to stay there till spring!"

11

Captain's Log: Stardate July 5, Sunday:

The pool was great! Next time we can bike there on our own. There were lots of kids at the fireworks show. They must live around here somewhere. . . .

P.S. Big question of the week—what is a projection? And what is going to happen tomorrow night at midnight?

"Is it time for the bus yet?" Josh's whisper floated toward me in the dark. I shone the flashlight on my watch.

"Eleven-thirty. Thirty minutes left."

Josh groaned and rolled over in his sleeping bag. "I can't stay awake much longer. Let's get out of the tent now."

"Do you know how many mosquito bites you could get in thirty minutes?"

Josh's flashlight snapped on. He shone it on his calculator and started pushing buttons.

"What are you doing?"

"I'm figuring out how many mosquito bites we could get in thirty minutes."

"You can't figure out a thing like that! You don't know how many mosquitoes are in the yard or how fast they bite or anything!"

"I'm making up numbers," he said calmly. "It's better than lying here watching your stupid watch." He pushed more buttons, mumbling to himself.

"All right," I said finally, trying to sound scornful instead of curious. "What numbers did you get? How many bites?"

"Well . . ." He looked down at his calculator like a scientist studying a very important problem. "I figured there's about a thousand mosquitoes on our lot."

"Oh, yeah?"

"But they aren't all in the same place. So I divided the yard into sections. I figured there'd probably be about thirty-five near us."

I groaned again.

"And on a warm night like this, they'd bite about every five seconds. So I—"

"You're crazy."

"I had to divide my answer by three, because a third of them would be busy biting Carrie, a third would get you, and the last third," he sighed, "would get poor ol' me. Hey," he shone the flashlight into my face, "do ghosts get mosquito bites?"

"Of course not!" Then I made my voice low and dramatic: "They have no blood. Heh, heh, heh."

"We'd better stay inside," Josh said with a giggle. "Because out there we'd get 6,480 mosquito bites by the time the bus got here. I bet you could *die* from that many bites."

"Then *we'd* have no blood. Heh, heh, heh." Then I changed back to my bossy voice. "Dummy, you can't figure it like that. Because mosquitoes don't just hang in midair and they probably can't hold that much blood, and Carrie'll have that repellent all over her, anyway."

"Then more of 'em will get her. They love that stuff. It's like ketchup on their hot dog."

"Hey, guys," Carrie's voice whispered outside the tent. "Come on out. It's almost time." She unzipped the flap enough to stick her head in. "Mom and Dad were so tired tonight, they conked out almost before Brooke. It was easy getting out."

"Is Brooke asleep?" I grabbed my binoculars and followed Josh out of the tent.

"I bumped her when I crawled out, and she started talking in her sleep again. She said, 'Please pass the window.'" Carrie giggled. So did Josh and me. We were all nervous, all wondering the same thing: What would happen when Aunt Vira and C.C. finally got here? What the heck was a projection?

"It's a good thing they're coming late this time so nobody else will see them." Then Carrie grabbed my arm. "Ryan, aim the binoculars over there! I think I saw a light!"

"It's not time yet!"

"Then they're early."

"It *is* them!"

"Come on!"

The night was darker than last time. The bus really looked like a UFO. And the bodies coming out the door were so glowy. Spooky.

C.C.'s voice broke the spell.

"I knew you'd be here!" She half ran, half glided toward us. "I can hardly wait to start!"

"Start what?"

"Aunt Vira and I have been planning all week how to do it," she went on eagerly. "She's read a bunch of psychic books. We've got it all figured out."

"Do *what*?" Carrie and Josh and I cried together.

"The projection!" C.C. answered impatiently. "What else? We're going to project ourselves past that intersection. And you're going to help."

"Psychic help," Aunt Vira spoke behind C.C. "I've been reading everything I can find on the occult. This sort of thing hasn't been done before, exactly—but I think we can modify the séance technique just a bit."

"Séance!" Josh took a step back.

"It won't be a real séance," C.C. explained. "Those are for getting in touch with ghosts. And you've already got ghosts. Two of them." She smiled at us. Her teeth glowed in the dark.

"But—" I started.

"It's just the procedure." Aunt Vira stared at us over her glasses. "You see, the barrier holding us back is psychic. So it requires psychic energy to get past it. And right at the scene of the accident is where C.C. and I are weakest. At the intersection of Highway 12 and Appleridge Road. We need your energy focused with ours to break past the barrier."

"We can . . . do that?" Carrie whispered. But Josh gave me a worried look.

"Psychic *what*?" he asked suspiciously.

C.C. sighed. "You don't know much about the occult, do you?"

"We haven't been shut up in a bookmobile all week reading about it," I shot back.

"I haven't either. Aunt Vira was the one doing that. I found something better." C.C. pulled a small paperback from the pocket of her windbreaker. "I finally found something worth reading. The only good book in the whole bus." She waved the flickery paperback at us. "It's a joke book. What do you get when you cross a—"

"About the projection," said Aunt Vira sternly, "I

think it would be best to have a little practice, to show you just what we're talking about. We can sit right here on the grass in a circle and lightly touch fingertips—"

"Uh-uh," Josh said in a low, stubborn voice. "Not me."

"Oh, come on," I said loudly to cover the funny feeling in my stomach. "It's only practice. Are you chicken or something?"

"It's not going to do anything to *you*," C.C. added. "Your clunky bodies will keep you right where you are. We're the ones who want to get projected."

"You do want to help C.C. and Aunt Vira to escape, don't you?" Carrie challenged Josh.

"Not if we have to do a creepy séance."

C.C. pointed a finger at Josh. "Methinks thou dost protest too much!"

"Off with your head," Josh replied calmly.

Aunt Vira sighed and pushed at her glasses nervously. "Children, children, if your psychic energies are scattered into quarrels, we'll never be able to summon enough power!"

"We'll do it." Carrie sat down on the grass and pulled Josh down with her by the shirt. "All of us." She leaned toward Josh's ear. "Quit acting like a baby."

"Off with *your* head."

Aunt Vira sighed again. "We can practice the procedure. Maybe that will reassure you. But the power will not grow if one of you resists." She raised her

71

hands. "We will all touch fingertips, like this."

Josh sat with his arms folded.

"He's just chicken," I said and flapped my elbows at him. "Bawk, bawk."

"Oh, yeah?" He grabbed my fingers hard enough to add them onto his own hand. "We'll see who's chicken!"

On my other side, a warm rush of air blew at my fingers where Aunt Vira's fingers touched mine. Goose bumps slithered down my neck. But I gritted my teeth. We'd just see who was chicken.

Aunt Vira spoke in a slow, soothing voice: "We must empty our minds of all distractions. We must have only one mental image. The intersection of Apple-ridge Road and Highway 12. We will try to picture the bus approaching the intersection. We will focus all our mental energy on this thought."

I could hear Carrie's slow, deep breathing. I sneaked a quick look at her face. It looked dreamy, tuned out. Just like when she was lost in a book.

"The intersection. Think of the bus approaching the intersection." Aunt Vira's voice was very slow, very soothing.

The warm air whooshed over my fingers. The rest of me felt colder all of a sudden.

Josh was right. This was creepy. And what good would it do, anyway, sitting on the wet grass muttering some mumbo jumbo? I mean, people couldn't really think themselves somewhere, could they?

"We will focus—"

"Carrie!" A new voice, from across the yard. Then louder. "*Carrie!* You out there?" Mom.

Carrie dropped her hands. She blinked. "I have . . . to go." Her voice sounded a little dazed. "Mom's calling."

"If she starts looking for you, she'll see all of us!"

"You'd better leave! Right now. Before she sees the bus."

Suddenly, everyone was moving and talking.

"We'll try again," Aunt Vira's voice whispered out of the darkness. "Next Monday."

"Carrie, did you hear me?" Mom's voice was closer. In a second, she'd be around the corner of the schoolhouse.

"Into the bus, C.C.!" Aunt Vira's voice was staticky, fading.

"Coming." Was that Carrie answering Mom, or C.C. answering Aunt Vira? I couldn't tell. The yard was all moving shadows and whispers. But I did hear C.C.'s voice one last time before I ran for the tent:

"We clicked. Just for a second. I felt it!"

12

"Something *did* happen. C.C. was right," Carrie said for the third time.

I gave another bang with the hammer. Just two more nails and the high jump frame would be finished.

Carrie thumped the Trixie Belden book in her lap. "The kids in my mystery books pay attention to strange feelings," she insisted. "And I have a strange feeling. Something's different."

"You're dumb. So's C.C." Today, in broad daylight, with ordinary weeds and grass and cornstalks everywhere, the thought of sitting in a circle touching fingertips like a bunch of loonies made my face red. Josh was right. That psychic business was bonkers. I banged in another nail.

"They'll never escape from here with that astrology stuff," Josh said, banging in a nail on his end. "What

74

they need is to fix the bus—get more power in it."

"Sure," said Carrie. "Fix a ghost bus. Should we tell them to bring it into the garage next Monday?"

I set the bamboo pole across the nails of the high jump frame. "There. Finished."

"Ooh," Carrie growled. "You two are hopeless. We have more important things to talk about than a stupid high jump! And anyway, if you want to build some-thing so much, you should help me with the tree house!" She stalked away and plopped down in the lawn chair, holding her book up in front of her face.

"The bus won't be back until Monday," I said. "We have the whole week to talk about it." Today I wanted to think about nice, ordinary, understandable things like high jumps. Things that didn't wiggle or glow or disappear. I wanted to forget the weird feeling in my stomach and the goose bumps that I had last night.

"We need some pads," I said, looking around. I can't do a Fosbury flop onto hard dirt.

"You aren't supposed to do Fosbury flops anyway," said Carrie, "They're dangerous."

"We can land in the strawberry bed," Josh sug-gested. "Dad's got so much mulch on it, it'd be as good as three mattresses."

"Sure. Then I'd have to mulch my rear end." I pointed to Dad's *Trespassers Will Be Composted* sign.

Josh jumped onto the tree swing. "Ryan, move the high jump closer," he called. "I just figured out a brilliant way to get over the pole." He pumped until his feet were almost level with the high jump pole. Then, on the height of the next swing, he let go and sailed right over the pole—and into the rhubarb patch.

"Uh-oh, wait till Daddy sees!" Brooke had a way of appearing like magic as soon as one of us was in trouble. "Wait till Daddy sees the new *rhu-barb!*"

Josh bent over the rhubarb. "Anyone got any pink duct tape?" He looked around desperately.

But it was too late. Dad was coming over.

"Joshua Walden Evans!" He stood with his hands on his hips, glowering down on poor Josh. "Would you kindly tell me what you are doing sitting in the middle of the new rhubarb?"

"Uh—"

A giggle sounded from somewhere behind me.

Josh glared at Brooke. "Shut up, blabbermouth."

"I didn't say anything!" Brooke yelled back.

"Sure. Sure. Liar."

"I *didn't.*"

"All right! That's enough!" Dad was yelling now, too. "Between you and the grasshoppers, I won't have any garden left." He shook his finger at Josh. "If sitting on the rhubarb is the only way you know to spend your free time, then maybe you don't need so much free time! See that marker? I'm going to put in a fruit tree. It'll need a deep hole. You all can take turns digging. Get busy!"

I grabbed the shovel. Then I took a closer look in Dad's wheelbarrow. "Hey, what's in there?"

Josh leaned over to look, too. "Yuk! It's hair!"

"Hair! Let me see!"

"Gross. Where'd it come from?"

"From the barber," Dad said irritably. "He saved it for me. It's good for the garden."

"He . . . *saved* it for you?"

"You didn't tell him your name, did you?"

"Does he have any kids in the fifth grade?"

Dad waved his trowel like a pointer. "It decomposes into nitrogen. For your information, seven pounds of hair have as much nitrogen as a hundred pounds of manure!"

"How many pounds of dandruff?" Josh muttered out of the side of his mouth.

"Yuk." Carrie scrunched up her face. "Did you ever get a hair stuck in your throat?" She shuddered. "I'll never eat another vegetable."

"Just put a little shampoo on it," Josh whispered.

"*Dig!*" Dad yelled. "Get busy! And try not to fall in the rhubarb on your way over there!"

"It's all your fault," I turned on Josh. "You and your brilliant ideas."

"He shouldn't have put the stupid rhubarb there in the first place," Josh grumbled. "Right next to the high jump." Then he hiccuped and started giggling again.

Dig, lift. Dig, lift. The shovelfuls of dirt got harder to lift as the hole got deeper.

"If we go any farther down, the stupid tree'll sprout

fortune cookies." I jabbed the shovel down into the hole.

There was a clink of shattering glass.

"What did you hit?" Josh bent over the hole.

"I don't know. Must be an old bottle or something."

"Wait." Carrie grabbed the trowel and leaned down into the hole, pawing at the dirt. "Looks like an old jelly jar. Or it was until you broke it."

"Why would anyone bury that?" People found old pop cans or beer bottles buried in dirt, not mason jars.

"There's something inside!" Carrie cried. Josh started digging from the other side. I reached down and carefully pulled the broken jar from the ground.

"There's an old newspaper or something inside!" Carrie's voice went up a few notches. "And coins!"

"We found buried treasure!" Josh cried, waving the trowel like a sword. "I bet pirates came by here a long time ago and dug a hole right here and hid golden coins and—"

"Don't be *dumb*. These aren't golden coins." I tipped them out carefully. "They're just dimes and nickels and quarters." I looked closer. "Old ones, too. Here's a buffalo nickel. 1915."

"This one's a dime. 1912." Carrie examined hers.

Now Josh was studying them, too. "The quarter has an eagle flying sideways," he reported. "1923."

"So who buried them, anyway?"

"Someone who lived a long time ago."

78

"But who? Why?"

"Maybe the paper says." Carrie reached her hand in gingerly past the ragged glass edges and pulled out the yellowed paper.

"Careful. It's so old, it'll tear easy."

"Move back. Quit shoving."

We all crowded around as Carrie carefully un-folded the paper. "The jar lid must have been on really tight all this time," she said. "If any water had gotten in, the whole paper would be rotten by now."

We spread it carefully on the ground and stared down at the faded picture of a lion jumping through a big hoop while a trainer held up a big whip.

Christy Bros. Big Five-Ring Wild Animal Show!
Five-Continent Menagerie!
Free Street Parade.
Two shows Daily: 2 & 8 P.M.
50¢ adults   25¢ children

The ad was yellow and faded and run through with crinkled lines, but still readable.

"It's an ad—for a circus. Or part of one, anyway." I knelt beside the paper, staring at the words. "But who could have buried it?"

"Must have been a long time ago, if it cost only a quarter."

"Hey, there's some writing on the back!" I could barely see the faded ink scrawls going sideways across

79

the paper. I practically had to push my nose down on the paper to decipher the words.

"It says, *Meeting time: one thirty Thurs . . . day.*" I squinted harder. "There's a date, too, but it's torn. Something *'nine'* then *'nineteen twenty-seven,'* I think."

Carrie bent over the ad beside me. "Look farther down. *G-A-N* . . . the last letter's a G, I guess. Yeah. *G-A-N-G*—Gang!"

I smoothed out the paper to read the faint words at the very bottom. "Hey, these are names! *Harry, John, Ty, and Wil*—something. The last part is torn." I set the paper down and rubbed my eyes. "That's all."

"Maybe it was a club or something. With those kids at the school," Josh said thoughtfully.

Carrie chewed her braid tips. "It's a clue. An important clue to something," she said in a hushed voice. "I know it. It's *evidence*."

"Two quarters. Four dimes. Two nickels. If kids' circus tickets cost a quarter, it'd be just enough money for four kids."

"I bet they were going to meet here. I bet they were going to dig up the money or something and go to one of the performances!"

"The two o'clock one."

Now even I felt like a detective. We'd figured it all out, just from that one old torn piece of paper.

"Don't tell Mom and Dad about it," Carrie said. "The kids in my detective books *always* keep their clues

80

a secret. They *never* tell grown-ups. We need to hide all this somewhere."

"Thursday, something nine, 1927." Josh turned the quarter over in his hand as he spoke. "There's only one thing that doesn't make sense. If they went to so much trouble to keep it safe in the jar—"

"Then why didn't they ever come back and dig it up?" finished a voice behind us.

13

"I missed my bus." C.C. grinned at the three of us, our mouths flapping open like fish.

"B-but," I sputtered. The weird feeling that had gurgled up in my stomach all morning was going to explode any second, like an appendix. "But—"

"Did Aunt Vira leave you?" Carrie whispered, wide-eyed.

"She didn't know that she did," C.C. answered smugly. "I mean, everyone was moving so fast, every which way. And she was so worried that your mom would see the bus. And I did go inside for a minute. But I felt different after our projection try. Stronger. Almost—liberated!" She turned a vapory cartwheel. "I was ready to try something new!" She looked thoroughly pleased with herself.

"So I said to myself, when Aunt Vira starts up the bus, when she's concentrating on her driving, then try to get out. It's one of the advantages of being a ghost. You don't really need doors."

"I *knew* something happened," Carrie cried. She waved the circus poster. "Two things! And last night was only a practice!"

"I broke free of the psychic gravity!" C.C. chanted it, like a poem. "Now if we could just get the whole bus free, just think of the places Aunt Vira and I could go!" She beamed at us. "Wait and see: Next time we'll summon up enough power to break the whole haunt pattern!"

"Won't Aunt Vira try to come right back for you when she finds out you're gone?" I asked.

"Well . . . she's got the whole bus with her, see? I don't think she could leave it, like I did. So it'll sort of weigh her down. Without me, she probably won't be able to get through to the real world till Monday, like usual." C.C. flopped down cross-legged in the dirt. "Meantime, here I am." She cocked her head to look at the poster. "I wonder why the kids who buried that never came back?"

My brain couldn't handle two problems at once. The ad would have to wait. "Look, we've got to find a place to hide you!" Dad and Mom and Uncle Doug were just inside the schoolhouse. If Aunt Vira wouldn't make it back until next Monday—

"Don't worry about me," C.C. said confidently. "I already found a place. That cute little outhouse over there. Just my size."

"Oscar's place?"

"Gross." Carrie wrinkled her nose. "Oh, C.C., don't stay there. It stinks. None of us go in there anymore, now that we have a real bathroom."

"I can't smell, anyway." C.C. shrugged. "When I need to hide, I can sit there and read my book. I brought my joke book." She reached into her windbreaker pocket and pulled out a little paperback.

"Oh, *no*," she cried. "How could I? I picked up Aunt Vira's quote book instead of my jokes! Now what am I gonna do?"

"You're gonna get someplace, quick!" Josh jumped up. "Here come's Norbert!"

"I forgot," I groaned, "Mom invited him for lunch."

C.C. half jumped, half glided into the tree just as Norbert started up the driveway with Brooke skipping along beside him.

"Lunch'll be ready in a jiffy," Mom called out. "You kids better wash up."

I looked at Josh, then at Carrie, then up at the tree, just a few yards from the picnic table. C.C. smiled and waved from her perch.

Things were getting complicated.

14

Norbert leaned back against the tree and blew on his coffee to cool it.

"Sun Valley Days is comin' up pretty soon. It's the big festival around these parts. Just like a carnival, with rides and goodies and game booths. You all should take the day off and go."

"We should," Dad said in that absentminded tone that meant he was really thinking about the schoolhouse or his September classes. Dad had a lot on his mind lately.

"Sounds like fun," I said, trying to look interested, to think about the people here at the table, not the ghost up in the tree.

"There's something else going on this weekend," Norbert went on. "The fiftieth reunion of my high school graduating class." He sounded excited. "We're havin' a fancy banquet dinner across town. All the old-timers that can make it back will be there. It'll be good to see 'em."

"Uh, speaking about carnivals and things like that," I said carefully, "did you go to circuses when you were a kid, Norbert?" If we could get Norbert talking about circuses, maybe we'd learn something about the old poster and coins. And with Norbert talking full speed, C.C. wouldn't have a chance to make trouble. Maybe.

"The circus? Now, that was the magic word when I was a boy." Norbert picked up his pipe. "The most excitement we had all year was when the circus came to town. Some of them wintered right up at Baraboo."

"How much did it cost to go to the circus then?" Josh asked, giving me a sideways look.

"Oh, about two bits. Of course, the parades were free." He stared down the road. "Part of the parade route sometimes went right down Highway 12, because the big top was set up at the edge of town."

"Did kids go from the schoolhouse to see it?" I tried to sound casual.

"Well, by the time the circus got rollin', school was about out for the summer. Of course, same as nowadays, friends saw each other over the summer." He stared out across the cornfield with that happy remembering look I was getting to know very well. "Never a dull minute when the circus was in town. One year, there was a baby elephant on the loose. Then there was the time one of the trapeze people fell and broke a leg. Another year somethin' spooked the horses in the parade, and we just about had a stampede." He shook his head.

"Funny thing, that. Some said there was a wild animal loose, scarin' the horses. Others said it was spooks." He winked. "Myself, I always thought *those* people had been celebratin' a bit too much with Mat Turner's bootleg whiskey, if you know what I mean."

"What do you mean?" Brooke asked innocently.

"Well . . ." Norbert sloshed the last of his coffee around in his mug, "what I mean is, when folks start seein' things that just ain't there, most likely they been drinkin'. There ain't no such thing as spooks."

I heard a suspicious sound overhead—like a snort. A branch sailed out of the tree, just missing Norbert's head.

"I heard a funny noise," Mom looked around with a frown.

"Some kind of bird, I guess," Carrie mumbled, staring hard at the table.

I groaned inside. All we needed was for Dad to get out the binoculars and start staring up into the tree.

Sure enough, he looked up, but just for a few seconds. "Might be that yellow-bellied sapsucker I saw this morning," he said in the same absentminded tone.

Josh nudged me. "More like a spook-bellied yaksucker," he whispered in my ear.

There was a muffled giggle from above. My stomach tightened around the peanut butter sandwich I'd had for lunch. I hiccuped.

87

"Drink some water," Mom ordered.

I hiccuped again. C.C.'s face peered down at me through the leaves.

> "You have to hold your breath while you drink it; three gulps without breathing,"

she whispered.

I looked quickly at Mom. She was still staring around the yard with that frown on her face. "Rob, you must have left the radio on."

"Mmmm," Dad was still deep in his own thoughts.

"Yeah, it's probably a radio," Josh said loudly. "Somebody'd better turn it *OFF*."

> "You may fool all the people some of the time. . . ."

came the breathy whisper from up in the tree. I could just barely see C.C., floating between two branches, bent over her book. I tried frantically to think of a way to shut her up, or at least drown her out. And then my heart sank. Brooke was staring up into the tree—

"Hey, is that—" she began. The same instant, Carrie jumped up and grabbed her by the hand, yanking her off the bench.

"Brooke, remember you wanted me to teach you a headstand?" she yelled. "Let's do one now."

> "You can even fool some of the people all the time. . . ."

88

Mom stood up, her hands on her hips. "There it goes again! That same static sound. Rob, don't you hear it?"

"What?" Finally, Dad was paying attention. "A funny noise?" He put his arm around her. "Well, Lynn, you know what Norbert says about people who see and hear things that aren't there." He grinned.

Norbert chuckled. Mom glared at Dad.

"For that crack, you get KP duty," she shot back, and tossed him the dish towel.

I heaved a sigh of relief when they walked away, then shook my fist up at the tree.

> "But you can't fool all of the people all the time."

C.C. ended cheerfully, waving her quote book, and then ducked back into the branches.

15

Captain's Log: Stardate July 8, Wednesday:

Code: TOPSECRET

*Buried poster and old coins now
hidden in Carrie's book box
in schoolhouse.*

Ghost hiding in outhouse.

I chewed my pen and stared at the logbook. It looked so simple on paper. It didn't even begin to describe the problems of having C.C. around. *Nothing* could describe them.

"I'm free! I'm free! We've biked four miles away from the schoolhouse. And this is a road Pegasine never even *went* on. I'm free of the haunt pattern path!" C.C. babbled on and on from the handlebars of my bike. She glanced back. "What's the name of this little road, anyway?"

"I don't know. The sign must have fallen down. It's just some road." I held the handgrips tightly. Sweat dripped from my forehead into my eyes, and it wasn't just from the heat. It's a very weird feeling to be biking along, trying to see past a ghost perched on the handlebars. Good thing it was just a skinny, unmarked country road, and that the cornstalks were getting so tall, and that Carrie and Josh were both biking on the outside to help hide us. I wished I'd never let C.C. talk me into her crazy idea of riding her on my bike. The sight of the red brick schoolhouse had never been so welcome.

"We'd better pull in at the back of the schoolhouse," Josh called out. He sounded worried, too. "In case Mom and Dad and Brooke are back."

I checked the driveway, shading my eyes with my hands, trying to see through—or around—C.C. No car parked there yet.

"They're still at Bill's, I guess." Mom and Dad had finally taken Norbert up on his offer to visit Bill's old barn full of antiques. "But stay out of sight, anyway!" I ordered C.C.

She didn't even seem to hear. "I'm free. I'm free!" she cried again and glided down onto the grass as I pulled into the backyard.

"Does that mean you're free for good from the haunt pattern?" Carrie asked, parking her bike.

"Well, of course I don't know *everything* about all this," C.C. admitted. "This is the first time I've been a ghost, you know. But at least it's a good first step. The next try should be farther—all the way into town. Like to that carnival." She smiled hopefully at me as she said it.

"No," I said quickly. "It's impossible."

"Mom and Dad still think you're a radio," Carrie explained. "We have to keep it that way."

"Well, how am I gonna find out how free I am unless I *go* places?" C.C. said with a loud sigh. "It's no fun trying by myself. And I need wheels to *really* travel. At least, I *think* I do."

"*No!*" Josh and I said at the same time.

"But I *like* carnivals!"

"We'd never be able to get you there, for pete's sake," Josh added.

C.C. folded her arms and glared at us. "If I *am* free, it's a big waste of time to stay in this boring yard all week until Aunt Vira brings the bus back!"

"When she does come back with the bus," Carrie said slowly, "and when you go back inside, will you be in the haunt pattern again?"

C.C. thought about that a minute. "We'll just have to do another projection," she said finally. "Get the whole bus free. It's the only way."

"But—"

"It'll work completely next time. I know it will," she

went on excitedly. "We're experts at it now. And just think of the places Aunt V. and I will be able to visit! It'll be just like we planned for her retirement, only better. In Pegasine instead of a van camper!"

She flipped back into a somersault and sat up grinning. "It's always been just Aunt Vira and me, you see," she explained. "She's taken care of me since I was a baby. We had all these summer trips planned all over the country. Now we can travel all year round once we get past that intersection. No school!" She back-rolled again. "I never could do back-rolls before," she called out on the way up. "I bet there are lots of things I can do now. I bet I have powers I haven't even figured out yet! You know, once I get the hang of it all, I think I'll like being a ghost. I'll bet it's *fun* to haunt things!"

I looked at her curiously. Funny—I'd never really thought about how it would *be*, being a ghost and all.

"If you really could haunt anywhere you wanted . . ." Carrie's voice got dreamy. "Then just *think*, C.C.! Hawaii or France or Hollywood or . . ."

"She should go to an old, creepy castle full of cobwebs," Josh said. He laid some strips of caps on the ground, then picked up his pogo stick. "That's where ghosts usually live. And they rattle chains. Get yourself some chains, C.C." He started pogoing toward the caps. *Bang!* "Got one," he called out, guiding the pogo stick toward the next strip of caps.

"Quiet! Do you want everyone in the whole county to know where we are?" I cried. Count on Josh to try and turn a pogo stick into a cap gun.

"You know," C.C.'s voice was a breathy, excited whisper, "the ghosts in those old castles could do all sorts of things. They could make things float across rooms. . . ." She shut her eyes and started swaying back and forth, chanting in a low, commanding voice: "Come to me . . . bi-cycle . . . come to meeeee."

"Oh, brother." Josh rolled his eyes.

C.C. glared at him haughtily. "I can see you don't take my psychic potential seriously! What about the ghosts in the stories you've read? They could put curses on people and—and—make people go nuts—and—and probably see into the future or past—"

"Hey, C.C., if you can see into the past, then you can find out why those coins and that circus poster were buried in the schoolyard," Carrie cut in. "That's our real mystery. And who those boys were. Maybe the circus poster is really a map to more buried treasure or something!"

"Well . . ." Suddenly C.C. didn't sound quite so sure. "These things take practice, you know. And I've only been a ghost for a few weeks really."

"Norbert might know about it. He went to this school," I said. "We could—"

"No!" Carrie stamped her foot. "I've *told* you and *told* you. You have to leave grown-ups out of things like this. Even Norbert. He'd probably tell Mom and

Dad, and they'd take it to an antique dealer or something and it wouldn't be *ours* anymore!"

A car honked in the driveway.

I jumped up. "Uh-oh, they're back! C.C., hide!"

Josh pogoed around the corner. "It's Norbert's old pickup. And it's loaded with junk. Looks like they brought the whole barnful back with them."

"Ryan! Josh! Carrie!" Dad's voice called out. "Where are you kids? We need help unloading."

"Coming," I yelled back. Then, to C.C., "Stay here. Don't let them see you."

"But—"

"Stay *here*." I started across the yard.

The back of Norbert's pickup was a jumble of chair legs, table legs, and dusty boxes full of old things.

"Bill's barn is an antique-lover's heaven." Mom beamed at me as she walked by carrying an old-fashioned mirror. "The *best* find was the old oak school desk. It'll look perfect in the living room."

Norbert heaved a box onto the ground. He lifted another box and nodded at me. "You're the one that likes space stuff, aren't you? There's some old comics in this box, along with the newspapers. Buck Rogers comics. He was the big spaceman hero back in the thirties."

I took the box. A cloud of dust blew into my face.

"Thanks," I coughed. I stared down at the torn cover picture of a man in a space suit holding out some kind of ray gun or something.

"They were Bill's comics, really. He was the space buff, like I told you."

"Ryan, can you get the desk down?" Mom called from the house.

I set down the comic and climbed into the back of the truck, stepping carefully between an old crank phone and a box of dishes. Then I stopped, left foot in midair.

C.C. was sitting in the back of the truck, behind the desk.

"How—how," I gulped. Words wouldn't come. Sweat suddenly prickled my armpits.

"A new ghost talent," she whispered. "You know—appearing out of thin air?" She grinned triumphantly. "I just figured out how to do it!"

"Well, disappear back into thin air," I hissed. "What if it had been Mom or Dad who climbed up here? Or Norbert? You could have given him a heart attack!"

"Ryan, Mom says to hurry up with the desk—" Josh climbed up behind me, then stopped when he saw C.C. "What are *you* doing here?" he croaked.

"C.C., this is no time for jokes," I pleaded. "Someone else will see you. Disappear. Vamoose. *Vanish.*" Norbert was on his way over. And now Brooke was skipping toward the truck.

C.C. just sat there calmly, smiling that maddening smile. "I'll go. Under one condition."

"What?"

"That you take me to that fair with you."

"What!"

"It's important. I had a premonition. A *dream*. And it had carnival things in it. Like crowds and cotton candy. It means something. I'm meant to go."

"Aha!" Josh waved his finger at her. "That's it! You just want the cotton candy!"

"I'll help carry stuff," Brooke called out. I heard her climbing onto the truck. "Oh, there's C.C.," she said in her loudest voice. "Hi, C.C."

My head buzzed. This couldn't be happening. Norbert heading toward the back of the truck, Brooke the Loudspeaker here beside me, and Mom and Dad walking across the yard toward us. I took a deep breath, then leaned down so my face was only a few inches from C.C.'s wavery one.

"If you don't disappear from this truck right now—" I searched frantically for a good threat for a ghost: "I'll—I'll stop talking to you. We'll all ignore you. And when Aunt Vira comes back, we won't help you escape!"

"Yeah," Josh added in his toughest voice. "Don't bite the hand of the horse that feeds you." Then he scratched his head. "Did I say that right?"

"And you're *not* going with us to the fair," I added. "So scram." It came out even meaner than I meant it.

C.C. stared back at me. Her eyes narrowed into

ghostly slits. "All right for you, Ryan," she said in a low, breathy voice. "All right for you. I'll disappear. For *now*. Just remember one thing. Ghosts don't just hide. Sometimes ghosts *haunt*."

16

"Last box," I called out. I took one last glance around the yard before stepping inside the doorway. No sign of C.C.—for now. She was probably sulking in the outhouse. An uneasy feeling chewed at my stomach. We had been kind of mean. . . .

"Thanks for helping to unload the stuff, kids." Mom picked up the desk and set it by the new window. She smiled at the room in general. "Can't you just *see* it? A blend of the new and the old. The living room there, the room divider there, and the kitchen over there."

I tried hard to listen, to think about something besides C.C.

"And the old wooden phone on that wall . . ." Dad put his arm around Mom. "And the bedrooms and bath downstairs."

"Oh, can't you just *see* it?" Mom said again. "With the carpeting . . ."

I looked around, following where they were pointing. For a second, all the lumber and tools and dusty boxes vanished. And I could almost see the furniture, the carpeting. It was the first time I'd really thought about the floor plan. It sounded kind of neat.

"The students' cloakroom used to be here in front. I got rid of it when I gutted the place. Their lunchroom was downstairs. The desks faced like this. . . ."

The lumber supplies disappeared again. But this time I saw desks, all in a row. And a blackboard. And kids, all ages, reading some old-fashioned books. And a frowning lady up front, with a hickory stick or something. And a dunce seat off in the corner. That's what they used back then, wasn't it? And lunch buckets with lard sandwiches, and chocolate iodine pills, and somebody out front with his tongue stuck to the pump.

Where had the boys who hid the jar sat? John and Harry and Ty and Wil—? Toward the back of the room, probably. Where they could whisper and make plans for their club and shoot spit wads. Did boys shoot spit wads then?

Dad shoved back a roll of fiberglass with his foot.

"But for now, we'll be lucky to have the basement partitioned and carpeted for winter." The faraway, dreamy sound left his voice. He sounded tired.

"Anything we can do?" I asked. Was that *my* voice volunteering?

100

Dad looked surprised. "As a matter of fact, yes. The insulation sale at the lumberyard starts tomorrow. Uncle Doug's coming by with his pickup. We'd like you kids to watch Brooke while we get the insulation. Thanks."

He looked at me and his tone changed. "Maybe soon we can stop all this work, work, work all the time and you kids will have more time for fun—to go to the park and meet other kids. There's just been so much to do. . . ." He shook his head.

He appreciated my "helpfulness." I felt a little smug.

Josh didn't appreciate it at all. He glared at me on the way out the door. "What'd you ask for more work for?" he hissed, then practically tripped on Brooke, who was running up the steps.

"Hey, watch where you're going, shrimp!"

She ignored him. "Ryan, guess what?" she cried excitedly. "My wart's almost off! Look! Mom said it's just hanging by a thread." She wiggled it back and forth for us.

Weird wart. The medicine must have only eaten away at the stem, leaving the rest of the wart flapping around like a loose tooth.

"Yep, hanging by a thread, all right." Josh nodded. Then he leaned closer to Brooke. "Just one teeny-tiny yank and it'll come off."

"No!" Brooke stepped back. "It'll hurt!"

Josh put his hands in his pockets and smiled a big,

devilish grin. He lowered his voice. "Brooke, I'll tell you a secret. If you pull it off and put it under your pillow, the wart fairy will come and leave you some money tonight."

I choked. Josh stepped on my foot.

"The wart fairy?" Brooke looked up at him, wide-eyed. "I never heard of a wart fairy."

"Well, most people just know about the tooth fairy," Josh went on in a low, confidential voice. "But she has a sister, see? The wart fairy. And she leaves more money."

"Really?" Brooke cried. "Really, Josh?"

"Yeah," I said. "Really." Now I was getting in the spirit, too. "But it's a secret about her, so don't tell anyone."

"You guys—" Carrie said in a warning voice. But Brooke took a deep breath.

"Well, maybe I will pull it off. But first I have to wiggle it some more." She skipped away, still wiggling.

"You and your big ideas!" Carrie put her hands on her hips. "Now what's she gonna do when she pulls the dumb thing off and sticks it under her pillow and it's still there in the morning?"

"Carrie," Josh said in an injured voice, "don't you believe in the wart fairy?" He shook his head sadly. I jabbed him in the side and ran down the steps, whistling.

But I stopped whistling as I got nearer to the outhouse. I practically passed by on tiptoe. No telling what kind of mood C.C. was in right now.

A voice rose over the outhouse roof—gloomy, ominous, threatening:

"I have not yet begun to fight."

17

I had this feeling all evening. A premonition, C.C. would have called it. Something was going to happen. I didn't know where C.C. was. But I could feel her around, being mad and bored and wanting revenge. And I could still hear her words: "Sometimes ghosts don't hide. Sometimes they haunt."

I stuck an extra piece of gum in my mouth and worked it around and around. Carrie and Josh were nervous, too. Josh dropped two plates while he was drying dishes. Then he got on his pogo stick and hopped around the yard.

Carrie sat and stared at her book for ten minutes without turning the page. Just sat there chewing her fingernails.

Only Brooke was happy and relaxed—and minus one wart.

"I'm going to fall asleep right away," she whispered

to me on her way to bed. "I won't peek when she comes."

"Who?" I asked, not really listening.

"The wart fairy!"

"Oh yeah. Her." I groaned inside. Carrie was right. It was a dumb idea. Now somebody was going to have to slip some money under Brooke's pillow, or we'd never hear the end of it.

Josh pogoed over to me. "Do you suppose C.C. will do anything?" he whispered, nodding toward Oscar's Place.

I shrugged. "She's just a dumb girl, you know." I blew a bubble, trying to look very confident and unconcerned. "And she doesn't even know very much about being a ghost. What could she do?"

"Right." He nodded. "Just a dumb girl. What could she do?"

I opened my eyes and lay in the pitch blackness of the tent, listening. And then I heard it again, a low moaning noise. Little shivers prickled my spine. I groped around for my flashlight, then shook Josh.

"Wake up!"

"Wha . . ." he mumbled, pushing me away.

"There's a noise. Right outside the tent. Listen."

We lay very still, hardly breathing, while my heart pogoed around inside my pj's. I heard another "Whoooo," then a muffled sound. A . . . giggle?

"Great," Josh muttered. "Guess who?" He shone

his flashlight on his watch. "Two in the morning, for Pete's sake."

I raised my voice to a loud whisper. "Is that you out there, C.C.?"

"I cannot tell a lie."

Then another giggle. Then a clanking sound. Then:

"Whoooooooooo . . ."

"I think she's trying to haunt us."

"Well, she's going to wake up Mom and Dad." I unzipped the tent and stuck my head out.

"Shut up out there!"

"Quoth the Raven, 'Nevermore.'"

returned the moaning, ghostly voice. Then another giggle.

I shook my fist into the darkness. "You'd better stop that if you know what's good for you!"

"An' the Gobble-uns'll git you ef ya don't watch out!"

There was another loud clang, then the sounds of rocks banging on the roof of the schoolhouse. Another "Whooooo." She was getting better at it.

"We've got to shut her up!" Josh said frantically.

"Throw my shoe over here," I whispered. "I'm going out."

But it was too late. There was a light on in the big

tent now. I heard voices; saw shadows moving. Any second now, Dad would be going outside to check.

I stuck my head through the door for one last warning. But my voice was drowned out by a loud shriek from the big tent.

"The wart fairy! I hear her! Quiet everybody—the wart fairy's coming!"

18

"I checked twice. There wasn't anyone out there," Dad said, turning his banana over and over in his hand instead of peeling it. "And there wasn't any damage at all. Not even a trash can kicked over. Nothing." He shook his head. "I thought at first it must have been some teenagers. They used to have beer parties here when the place was abandoned."

"But we didn't hear any car engines." Mom stood with her hands on her hips, looking from the driveway to the house to the street. "Maybe we should have called the police."

"The police!" Carrie gasped. I didn't dare look at her or Josh. But my eyes scanned the yard, searching. C.C. was lurking around somewhere, all right. Probably gloating over last night. Or studying the stupid quote book for more brilliant lines. If Aunt Vira didn't come back and fetch her soon, ol' C.C.'d be a twice-dead ghost.

Dad shook his head. "What could we say to the police? There's no evidence, no damage. We don't even all agree on what we heard. No, I think it was probably just some kid who didn't know there was anyone living here."

Just then, I noticed a suspicious, glowy form peeking around the corner of the schoolhouse. My mouth tightened.

"Right," I said loudly. "Probably just some dumb kid bumping into things in the dark."

Dad gave me a strange look. "Are you talking to us or the people in the next town?"

"Anyway," Mom said, "whoever it was, we probably scared them worse than they scared us."

"Brooke scared them away, you mean." Josh jumped up and danced around, flapping his arms. "The wart fairy, the wart fairy," he cried in a squeaky, high-pitched voice.

Brooke set down her cereal spoon. "She didn't come," she said in a quivery voice. "I looked and looked under my pillow and under my sleeping bag. I couldn't find any money and I couldn't find my wart." A tear rolled down her cheek.

Mom sighed. "Brooke, where in heaven's name did you ever get this wart fairy idea?"

"Josh told me about her," Brooke said, still sniffling. "He said she's the tooth fairy's sister."

"Oh, he did, did he?" Dad said.

Josh was suddenly very busy with his cereal.

"Well, Brooke," Mom said, staring hard at Josh, "I think Josh gets a little confused sometimes. And I think this was one of those times, right Joshua?"

"Mmm," Josh mumbled, red-faced.

Dad looked from Brooke to Josh and got up, shaking his head. "I'm going to work in my garden. After that 'restful' night last night, I need to relax. Kids," he said, stomping away.

Brooke wiped her nose on her sleeve. "Maybe the wart fairy thought I was sleeping inside the schoolhouse," she said in a trembly voice. "Maybe she left my money there." She got up and headed slowly toward the school, scuffing her feet in the dirt. Mom watched her go.

"That child and her imagination! Wart fairies, ghosts named C.C., icicle ladies. What next!"

"Grasshoppers! Everywhere!" Dad yelled from the garden. "Thousands of them. The carrot tops look like spiderwebs, they're so chewed up!"

"Why don't you look in your organic gardening book, Rob," Mom called, hurrying over. "There must be some way to get rid of them."

"Don't one of you fire until you see the whites of their eyes."

The voice came slowly, dramatically, from behind the schoolhouse.

"Everywhere I step, a bunch of them jump out," Dad cried. "It's like a plague."

"Speaking of jumping—look what I've got." C.C.'s voice sounded gleeful.

My head jerked up. There she was, peeking around the back of the schoolhouse.

"Oh, no," Josh groaned. "She's got my pogo stick!"

"Get back, C.C.," Carrie called softly, urgently. "Mom and Dad are just across the yard!"

"Back," Josh echoed. "Back, back, *back*!"

"Wait. I have a new trick to show you." C.C. climbed on the pogo stick, holding out one wavery arm to the schoolhouse wall for balance. "I used to know how to ride one of these, but it's tricky when you don't weigh anything."

"Didn't you hear what Carrie just said!"

"But I haven't shown you the best part yet! Remember I just learned how to turn invisible? Well, watch this," she bragged. And then, before our very eyes, she slowly blurred, like a picture out of focus, fading to nothingness, leaving the pogo stick standing up all by itself.

Then the pogo stick started moving.

Shivers ran down my back and up my neck. Carrie gasped and clapped her hand over her mouth.

"Holy cow," Josh murmured, wide-eyed.

"Pretty good, huh?" said the nothingness from the pogo stick.

111

Instead of its usual up and down jumping motion, the pogo stick was almost sliding across the grass in little, bumpy steps.

"Since I don't weigh anything, I can't make it really *bounce*, of course. But I think I could hit the caps with it—"

"*No*, C.C.! You have to hide or disappear or something!"

"Mom and Dad would never understand about a walking pogo stick," Carrie's voice squeaked a little.

"And they're coming *back*," Josh gulped.

"Okay, just one last jump here . . . uh-oh. Timmmber!"

And the pogo stick crashed down. "Stupid rock," came C.C.'s voice from the grass. "That's what tripped me. I—"

"*Shut up*," I said between clenched teeth. It felt very strange to be talking to a pogo stick. "They're coming!"

It didn't really *look* wrong. I mean, the pogo stick was just lying in the grass. And C.C. was still invisible. Then why was my heart beating so fast and scared? If only we could make her voice disappear, too.

"Stay invisible, C.C.," Carrie warned softly as Mom and Dad walked toward us.

"Well, much as I dislike the idea, I guess I'll have to use some kind of pesticide," Dad said. "Otherwise, the grasshoppers will get the whole crop."

"I wonder how high this pogo stick would
bounce if I dropped it from the roof. . . ."

breathed a ghostly voice right beside us.

"You wouldn't dare!" Josh said.

Dad's mouth fell open. He stared at Josh. "I didn't
realize you felt so strongly about pesticides," he said.
"Or is it that you're especially fond of grasshoppers?"

Josh look confused. "No, uh, I mean—"

"He was talking to me," I cut in quickly. "He, uh—
we were making a dare."

"I see." Dad didn't look completely satisfied.

I clenched my fists hard in my lap. Too bad they
didn't make muzzles for ghosts. Why couldn't she keep
her mouth shut!

"Let's get the lunch dishes cleaned up before Uncle
Doug gets here with the pickup," Mom said, setting
the dishpan on the table. "Pass your plates down, kids."

"This pogo stick's *great*. Where are the caps?
I want to play that cap game,"

C.C. whispered.

"You can't have them!" Josh cried.

This time both Mom and Dad stared with open
mouths. "I beg your pardon, Joshua," Mom said slowly.
"Why can't I have the plates? Do *you* want to do the
dishes?"

113

Josh was going to explode in about two seconds. One look at his red face and the boiling mad look in his eyes told me that.

"Josh, pipe down," I said, trying to gloss over the whole thing. "You're not funny, you know."

C.C.'s voice sounded different, surprised:

"Hey! I think . . . I see Pegasine coming!"

"Darn it, I just heard that staticky sound again," Mom said. "I'm going to find out once and for all where it's coming from!"

"Maybe that's what you heard." Dad pointed to Uncle Doug's pickup, turning the corner. "Doug's here."

C.C. gave a little squeal:

Pegasine is here, too—way down the road.
She's coming! And it's not even Monday!"

"Oh no! It's too early!" Carrie whispered. But Dad heard. He slammed his fist on the table.

"What in the world is the matter with you kids today? Just *why* is it too early for Uncle Doug to come?"

"Uh—because the dishes aren't done," I said quickly.

Dad looked from me to Josh to Carrie to Uncle Doug, just pulling into the driveway.

"There's something funny going on around here this morning," he said in a very calm, measured tone.

"Are you ready to go to the lumberyard?" Uncle Doug called out.

I glanced down the road out of the corner of my

eye. There was a familiar-looking blob of light moving in the distance. If it got much closer—

"Don't worry about a thing, Dad," I said quickly. "We'll clean up and we'll watch Brooke. We'll be just fine." I talked loud and fast, trying to keep one eye on the road and the glowing light, rolling closer with each second. I felt like pushing Mom and Dad into the truck.

"Sure, Dad," Carrie added. "We'll be fine." Josh just sat there, scowling at the pogo stick. He hadn't even noticed the bus.

"It's only for a few hours," Mom said. "The kids will be okay. I think they're just wound up about that carnival tomorrow."

"That's it." Carrie and I both nodded. "We're wound up about the carnival."

Dad stood there a moment, looking at us. Then he grabbed his shirt off the table. "All right," he said. "We'll go. But you behave yourselves! No monkey business, hear?"

The pickup pulled away down the road in one direction just as the glowing bus rolled down the hill from the other direction.

"Come on!" C.C. yelled, running across the yard, becoming more visible by the second. "Aunt Vira's back. Now we can try a *real* projection!"

19

"C.C.! What happened? Where have you been!" Aunt Vira was already out of the bus and hurrying across the yard. She look worried, happy, relieved, and mad all at the same time. Aunts are aunts, ghosts or not. "I've been trying and trying to get back through to you. It's so hard with the bus. I've been worried sick."

"I'm okay, Aunt Vira. Really. I've been here the whole time."

"I'll say," I muttered.

"Haunting us," added Josh, "with *quotes*." He grabbed the book out of C.C.'s hand and flipped through the wavery pages. "Aha! Here's one for you:

> 'From ghoulies and ghosties and long-
> leggety beasties and things that go bump in
> the night, Good Lord, deliver us!' "

116

He shut the book. "So there!"

"Beasties!" C.C. cried. "Ghoulies! I'll tell you who the beasties are. They're people who make other people stay in outhouses and don't let them talk—"

"If you could keep your mouth shut, you wouldn't have had to stay in the outhouse."

"Things that go *blab* in the night—"

"Children, children," Aunt Vira cried, holding up her hand. "It took me twelve hours of complete concentrated effort and all the psychic power I could muster to manage to bring the bus through to the physical world on a Thursday. I almost didn't make it. And I did not go to all that trouble just to be on hand for your quarreling. We have much more important things to do." She pulled out her astrology book. "Listen:

> 'Scorpios: Today is a day for trying new
> endeavors, for breaking out of old routines.
> Anything might happen.'

You see!" She held the book aloft like a torch or sword. "Today is a very significant day. The forces in the stars helped me to break through the haunt pattern to come to you today. I'm convinced of it. And those same psychic powers will continue to work for us as we try again."

"You mean . . . try the projection . . . again?" Carrie's voice was low, respectful.

"New places, new endeavors!" C.C. cried. She sounded eager and excited. Not mad anymore. "Oh, Aunt Vira, you're right! That's probably what my premonition was trying to tell me! That today's the day the projection will work! Let's start right now!"

"Not that fingertip mumbo jumbo again. Uh-uh. No way." Josh took a step back. C.C. ignored him.

"We should do it in the bus," she said eagerly. "If we're all inside, our psychic power will be more concentrated. And it's the bus that always gets stuck at the intersection, anyway."

I glanced over at the not-quite-real bus parked by the edge of the lot. In the daylight, it was like a glowing blob of shimmery air. Climbing into that would be like trying to high jump a sunbeam. I opened my mouth. But Aunt Vira spoke first.

"I don't know, C.C.," she said nervously. She adjusted her glasses and pushed back a loose hair. "I've been doing more reading on this. It might be risky. You see, if the bookmobile does get past the intersection, we'll be cutting the ties that hold us to this place, here and now. We could be flung anywhere. We're just spirits, remember. We're not bound to any place or any time—except by the haunt pattern. We'll be taking a risk in the bus."

My heart flopped. I glanced at Carrie. Her eyes looked about ready to turn over in their sockets.

"Any . . . where," she whispered. "Any . . . time?"

"It could happen," Aunt Vira answered solemnly.

She pressed her lips together for a moment. "I just can't be sure. You see, this is all so new to me—"

"But that's great!" C.C. cried, throwing out her arms. "That's the best news we've had in weeks! New places, new endeavors, just like our horoscope says! What are we waiting for? Let's get started, before your folks get back!" She started toward the bus.

"Hey, wait a minute," I yelled after her. "We can't go in there. It's not even solid."

She spun around. "How do you know you can't? You haven't even tried."

"Right." Josh nodded. "And we're not gonna."

"Well, if you're *chicken* . . ." She started walking, head high. "I suppose Aunt Vira and I could try it alone. After all, our power *is* growing. We're getting braver and stronger, too."

"We're not chicken. We're bodies. Solid. And this bus is a ghost."

She didn't turn around. Just flapped out her elbows. "Bawk, bawk, be-*bawk*."

I set my jaw. I wasn't going to let any ghost girl flap her wiggly elbows at me and call me chicken. I started toward the bus, walking fast.

"Ryan—"

"So who's afraid of an old ghost bus? Not me."

"Right." Josh caught up with me. His voice didn't sound as confident and loud as usual. I wondered if his heart was doing Fosbury flops, like mine.

"What about Brooke? We're supposed to be watch-

119

ing her," Carrie cried, running after us.

"That's right," Josh nodded. "We can't leave Brooke!" I looked at him suspiciously. Since when was he so worried about babysitting?

"You won't go anywhere. Your bodies will hold you back. So you won't be far from Brooke." C.C. turned around, friendly again. "I knew I could count on you guys!"

"Well, I suppose Caddie Woodlawn . . . or . . . Trixie Beldon would have . . . gone in. I mean, it's no worse than untamed wilderness . . . really." Carrie was chewing her fingernail so hard, her whole finger was practically disappearing.

If I hadn't been walking so fast, if it hadn't been a dare, I would have about-faced when we reached the glowing bookmobile. But momentum kept us going. That and the smug look on C.C.'s face.

I took a deep breath. One, two, three, *go.*

20

It felt like I was walking through a wall of snow. Snow that wasn't cold. Snow that got in my hair, my eyes, my mouth, my arms.

"Yuk! This stuff's all over me!" Carrie thrashed her arms at it. "What did we come in here for, anyway?"

"Dear Lord, preserve us from ghoulies and ghosties and long-leggety beasties and things that go bump in the night," Josh muttered. It sounded like a real prayer this time.

And then we were through. And I suddenly knew how Captain Kirk and his crew felt when they boarded alien crafts.

"Holy cow."

"It isn't like untamed wilderness. It's like . . . it's like . . ." Carrie whispered.

It was like being underwater. Everything was all wavery. The books swaying in their shelves, the walls, the ceiling, the floor. And the big, shiny, stuffed unicorn, bobbing from the ceiling like an alien creature, pointing its horn at us.

"We just did an incredible feat," Josh mumbled. "First kids to be ghostified."

He looked fluorescent. So did Carrie. "Wow," she said. Then she said it again. "Wow." She reached over carefully to touch the shelves of wavery books. "Hey, there's *The Wizard of Oz!* Is *Trixie Belden* here, too? And *Caddie?* Are they all ghost books?"

"We're not here to read, for Pete's sake!" I pulled her away from the shelves.

"Well." Aunt Vira looked at us all standing inside the bus. "C.C. was right; the power is more concentrated inside Pegasine. I can feel it already." Her voice sounded hollow, echoey. "With all our thought power joined, we have a good chance to escape. But much of my own power has already been drained by breaking through to you today. I'll have to rely on you children."

"Uh-uh. Not that thought power stuff," Josh said. His voice was somewhere between stubborn and panicky. He walked slowly to the front of the bus, almost swimming through the ghost air.

"Look," he said, "you're doing this all wrong. It's the bus that needs more power."

"A lot you know about ghostmobiles," C.C. scoffed, leaning back against the shelves. "This one's moved by psychic power, not gasoline."

"It has an engine, doesn't it?" I demanded. "And Aunt Vira sits at the wheel and drives, doesn't she?" I touched the dashboard cautiously. The key was in the ignition.

"Boys, I wish you'd move back just a little," Aunt Vira said, fiddling nervously with her glasses. "You see, there's no solid matter weighting the bus engine anymore. The slightest pressure on that pedal . . ."

I stared at the pedal with new respect.

"C.C.," Aunt Vira was really going to wear out her nose, pushing her glasses up and down it so often, "C.C., maybe this wasn't the best idea, working inside Pegasine."

"It *is* the best idea!" C.C. spun around. Her eyes were glowing like cat's eyes. "There's much more power here. We're making our own psychic force field."

"That's what I mean." Now Aunt Vira was cracking her knuckles, or trying to. Ghost knuckles couldn't crack. "This power—we don't really understand how it works. And I don't want anyone getting hurt."

"We just have to do like last time, Aunt V. Everything will turn out fine." C.C. put her arm around Aunt Vira's shoulders, talking calmly, reassuringly, like she was the elderly aunt. "We'll be able to break free this time. I know it!"

"But C.C., it's not that simple. In these sorts of cases of ghostral projection, the direction of our thoughts will determine the direction of the bus. And we're hardly trained in psychic disciplines—"

123

"Hey, what about us?" I said slowly. "We're not ghosts. What will happen to us if the projection works this time?"

"I told you. Your bodies will hold you back!"

Josh put his hands in his pockets and stared at C.C. stubbornly. "Thoughts don't take you places."

"Oh, come on, Josh," Carrie said. "It's not going to kill you to try it. You do want C.C. and Aunt Vira to escape the haunt pattern, don't you?"

"Then I wouldn't be around to bug you anymore." C.C. gave him her sweetest smile.

"Come on," Carrie said again.

Josh looked at me. So did C.C. and Carrie. They were all waiting to see who I sided with.

I chewed my lip. I looked out the window, then back in the bus, then at the driver's seat.

What had Aunt Vira said? "We will break our ties to this place. This time. We could be flung anywhere." The Enterprise crew never would have passed up a chance like this. I cleared my throat.

"Might as well try it." I tried to sound offhand. "I mean, we've gone this far. Might as well finish."

Josh plopped down, scowling. "Then let's get it over with."

"Great! Everybody on the floor!"

We made a strange-looking group: Josh sitting all straight and mad; C.C. with her face scrunched up, concentrating; Carrie chewing her fingernails; and

Aunt Vira perched in the driver's seat like a pilot waiting for the countdown.

"Now, we must first clear our minds." Aunt Vira's voice was firm and businesslike.

One second, two, three. I tried to clear my mind. But I just kept seeing the bus rolling slowly down the street, leaving Carrie and Josh and me sitting cross-legged in mid air in the middle of the road. A giggle popped out.

"Get serious!" C.C. fixed me with her sternest glare.

"I'm trying to!" I shut my eyes again. One second, two, three. Half a minute, a minute—

I opened one eye. Josh had his eyes open, too. We looked at each other. "See?" he muttered. "I told you it wouldn't work!"

"We did better than this in our practice!" C.C. threw up her arms dramatically. "We'll never escape at this rate. You guys aren't trying!"

"If only we had something solid, tangible," Aunt Vira said, tapping the steering wheel. "A visual focal point to act as a link."

Josh folded his arms across his chest. "One more time," he said. "I'll do this silly thing one more time."

"Yeah," I nodded. Maybe Josh had the right idea, after all. I mean, believing that a starship can take you all over the galaxy is a different thing than believing in a ghost bookmobile that doesn't even have a real engine.

125

"All right, children. This time I'll try directing the focus more with my voice. I want you all to fix a picture of the intersection in your mind." Now Aunt Vira was using the kind of voice that hypnotizers use: slow, sleepy. "Think of Appleridge and Highway 12. Picture us heading toward it."

Appleridge. Highway 12. Not starships. Not Kirk and the Enterprise.

"Picture the bus rolling slowly down the road between the cornfields. Picture the intersection right up ahead."

The intersection. It did have cornfields on both sides. And in a little while it was supposed to have a ghost bus whizzing by.

"Picture us getting closer, approaching this intersection." The voice was low, soothing, drowsy. The smallest tingle buzzed my fingertips. I swallowed hard. Was something starting? My fingertips buzzed again, like a small electric shock. I wanted to pull my hand away. But it felt fused to Carrie's.

Another tingle. This one was a real jolt. My mouth was very dry.

"Hey, everybody, don't leave me! I want to come, too!" Brooke burst through the door, one hand waving a piece of yellowed paper, the other holding her lard pail. I could hear something rolling inside it.

"Look what I found!" she cried. "The wart fairy did come. She left me lots of money and this picture, too. It was in Carrie's book box!" She held up a paper.

"A circus picture!" Part of it tore loose and fell on the floor.

It was like coming out of a deep sleep. My mind wouldn't work. For a second, we all sat there like hypnotized dummies, staring at the tattered poster.

Lions, cages. The circus. She had *our* poster. I wanted to yell at her. But I could only sit there, staring at those cages. Circus . . . circus . . .

There was a fuzzy-sounding rumble somewhere in the front of the bus. And then a weird, rocking feeling. C.C.'s voice broke through the haze. "It's working! We're moving!"

Moving? What was going on? I tried to get up. But my left foot was asleep, and I fell on Carrie.

"Get off me!"

"Move your big foot!"

"I'm trying!"

"We're moving!"

I could hear rushing air, hear the ghost engine straining, feel the speed, the vibrations. The dizzy feeling was like being sucked inside some stormy place, faster every second, whirling, tumbling, spinning.

Was this projection? If so, then Aunt Vira and C.C. were wrong. Our bodies weren't holding us back at all. Wherever the bus was headed, it was taking us along, too.

21

"Help!" Brooke yelped from the floor. "I'm allergic to going fast!"

"Stay down."

"What's happening?"

"We're falling!"

"Remain calm, children. The only thing we have to fear is fear itself." But even Aunt Vira sounded a little hysterical.

"Are we past the intersection?"

"I don't know."

"I want to go home!"

"Shut up, Brooke." Dummy Brooke and her wart fairy. With *our* poster and *our* money. She wasn't even supposed to be part of all this. Always butting in where she didn't belong, wrecking everything.

I grabbed the edge of the bookshelf with both hands

and tried to pull myself up to see out the door window.

The bus lurched again. I heard a loud, protesting rumble from the engine. And a high-pitched squeal from Brooke.

"Hey, we're still here!" She'd already made it to the window. "There's our schoolhouse!"

"What!" Everyone tumbled toward the door window. "Move over. Let us look!"

The gauzy ghost stuff was not as clear as a regular window. I practically went cross-eyed, squinting to see better.

There was a building outside.

The schoolhouse.

Only . . . different. I squinted harder. The bricks were different. Redder. The trim was different. No dirt driveway. No high jump stand. Dirt road under the bus instead of blacktop. And the yard . . .

There were different trees. Smaller. And a hilly dirt lot back where Dad's garden should have been.

"It's all wrong," Carrie breathed. "What happened?"

"Quit crowding!" Brooke tried to shove in between Carrie and me. "I was here first!"

"Wait a minute." I kept staring. A strange, tingly feeling prickled down my spine.

"It's the same place," Aunt Vira murmured, "but . . . newer. . . ." She looked around the bus, then picked up the poster lying torn and dirty on the floor.

"The direction of thought should determine the direction of the bus," she said, frowning. "And we were all staring at this—"

"Somebody moved the cornfield!" Brooke yelped. She was kneeling on Aunt Vira's seat, staring out the driver's window. "Where'd it go?"

"Just a moment, dear," Aunt Vira said absently, still peering down at the poster. "Nineteen twenty-seven," she murmured. "Could . . . *this* have been the focus? Could we have moved in . . . time?"

The bus rumbled again, then lurched, throwing us to the floor in a tangle of real arms and legs and whooshy ghost bodies.

"Help! Get off me!" C.C. screeched from the bottom of the pile. "You're crushing my poor nothingness!"

"You're tangled in my shirt!"

"Your arm went *through* my shirt."

"We're not going anywhere! I'll drive us. What does this pedal do?" Brooke's voice.

My head jerked up. Brooke was still in the driver's seat, her hands on the steering wheel, her body scooted down, as her foot reached toward the pedal.

"No!" I hollered.

"Leave that pedal alone, child! There's no telling what could happen at this point!" Aunt Vira cried.

Suddenly everyone was thrashing wildly to get up from the floor. Aunt Vira raced by in a rush of air.

130

But Brooke's red and blue tennis shoe with the big hole in the toe hit the pedal first.

There was a mighty rumble. The bus lurched forward. But this time I grabbed the shelf in time to keep from falling back down to the floor. The school yard was rushing toward us as Pegasine careened like a drunk through the yard.

"Stop her, Aunt Vira!" I yelled, staggering toward the front.

"I can't see where I'm going! I'm not high enough!" screamed Brooke.

"Our thoughts are chaos. We have no focus!" Aunt Vira grabbed the wheel just as a figure emerged from the bushes of the hilly back lot. A boy—wearing a cap and funny knee-length pants.

"*Brake!* There's someone coming!"

Aunt Vira's foot hit the brake. Pegasine reared like a spooked horse and pulled to a stop—just in front of the boy.

For a frozen second, we all stared at each other through the window. The boy opened and shut his mouth like a fish. He took a small, stiff step backward, then another, and another. Then he turned and *ran,* scrambling across the yard, thrashing through the bushes.

He tripped; something fell from his hand. Something that flashed in the sunlight as it tumbled down the hill into the weeds. But the boy didn't stop to get it. He scrambled back up and tore off into the field.

"Did you see the look on his face?" Josh's voice shook a little. Then he fell against the shelf as Pegasine shuddered with the mightiest rumble yet and lurched toward the hill.

"Dear me. *Dear me.*" Aunt Vira pulled hard left on the wheel. The bus veered sideways in a rocking drunken swing.

"What's going on?" C.C. yelled.

"I don't know. Pegasine has never acted like this before." Aunt Vira's voice was wild-edged. She pulled hard on the wheel again. "Concentrate, children. Concentrate! We need focus!" She yanked again. Pegasine swung the rest of the way around, throwing us against the opposite wall. Then, with a great wheezing rumble, she charged back across the yard—and out into the street.

22

"This is *it*! This is *it*!" C.C. cried, staggering to the front. "Thataway, Aunt V.! We're on the road!"

"We're going fast!" Brooke bounced up and down excitedly. "The wheels on the bus go 'round and 'round, 'round and 'round—"

"Quiet!" C.C. pulled Brooke off the driver's seat. "You stay down here. You're not going to flub this one!" She turned to me. "This kid needs a leash! Does she always do things like this?"

"All Scorpios do!" Josh called from the back.

"Concentrate, children," Aunt Vira hunched over the wheel. "We're heading toward Appleridge. This could be the moment we've all been waiting for!"

Appleridge and Highway 12, the fatal intersection. I swallowed hard.

"Keep going! Don't slow down!"

"Put the pedal to the metal!"

My heart was racing almost as fast as the bus. We all held our breath, watching, waiting as Pegasine rumbled down the dirt road. Except for the strange muffled noise of the ghost engine, there was complete silence inside the bus.

And then I heard it. Faint, faraway music.

"Hey," Carrie said slowly, cocking her head. "What's that noise?"

"Sounds like . . . music. Band music."

"Where's it coming from?"

C.C. saw it first. "Look!" she cried, pointing up ahead. "There's a bunch of people in the street! And animals!"

The scene raced into view—People, fancy wagons, animals marching in a great column down Apple-ridge, turning the corner onto Highway 12, toward town.

"A parade!" yelled Brooke. "It's a *circus* parade! There's a clown! And an elephant!"

And we were racing right toward it.

"Slow down, Aunt V.," C.C. cried, "or we'll run right into them!"

The music grew louder.

"We're going to crash!" Carrie shrieked.

"Put on the brakes!" I yelled. Old Pegasine was going to have another accident, and this time there'd be six ghosts on board.

Aunt Vira sat very straight, holding the wheel in a death grip.

"When the going gets tough, the tough get going," she said grimly. "We have reached the point of no return."

"But we want to return!" Josh yelped. "This isn't the right place and—hey, *look out*!"

The intersection. I braced myself, holding onto the wavery shelf for dear life. But instead of crashing into the parade, we slammed to a stop as if we'd hit a wall.

And the world slowed down. The acrobats' cartwheels became slow, lazy; the jugglers' balls stayed in the air too long; the red and blue and gold circus wagons moved as if in a slow-motion movie or a dream.

And like in a dream, we were struggling furiously and not going anywhere. Pegasine strained, churning power; Aunt Vira pumped the accelerator desperately. "Come *on*!" she cried.

"You can do it, Peg, ol' girl," C.C. called hoarsely. "Get across. *Do it*!"

"Go, go, *go*!"

The next second, there was a great ripping sound, as if the air itself was tearing apart. Pegasine shot forward. My ears popped like two baby cannons. A shock like electricity jolted the bus. Then came a sickening, falling sensation—

"Help! Catch me!" Brooke's voice. A shriek. Carrie? I clutched at the air, trying to grab something to break my fall. But there was just that warm snowy stuff all around me.

I heard horses neighing, elephants trumpeting.

135

The rest of the world had sprung back to life. But I was still in a slow-motion dream place. Falling . . . falling . . .

"Something's spooking the horses!" cried a faraway voice. "Hold onto the horses!" Then another voice, closer, high-pitched with excitement.

"We're doing it! We're getting through! Bye Josh, Carrie! Bye Ryan. Bye Pest! *Byeee*!" Then C.C.'s voice and Pegasine's rumble faded away, too. And still I was falling in my slow-motion dream fall while the parade sounds grew fainter and fainter. Was this how astronauts felt when they were tumbling around in zero gravity?

It was a dream. Had to be. Rolling, rolling, falling, falling. Falling through more than just air, and like in a dream, never reaching the—

I hit something hard.

"Ow!" Brooke's yell sounded curiously far away. "I fell on my knee."

For a second, I didn't answer. I just lay there and let the world spin around me like a merry-go-round.

I opened my eyes slowly.

Carrie was sprawled on one side and Josh and Brooke on the other. On blacktop, not dirt.

"What . . . the heck . . . happened?" Josh sounded spaced-out. He sat up slowly, rubbing his eyes, staring.

I stared, too. At the cornfields lining the street on both sides. Ordinary cornfields. No parade. No circus

136

pulling away down the highway. No ghost bookmobile.

"The c-circus," Carrie stammered. "The . . . bus. It's all g-gone. Did we . . . fall out?"

"We were zooming along . . . toward the intersection," Josh said in a funny dazed voice, "and then—whammo!"

"They got through," I said. I felt as spaced-out as Josh and Carrie sounded. I rubbed my eyes again, as if by squinting hard enough I could somehow see where it all went.

"And . . . we're back," Josh said in the same funny voice. "I think." He shut his eyes for a second, then opened them and looked around. He nodded. "Yep. We're back." He wriggled his mouth and thumped his ears like they were clogged. "Oh, boy."

"It's our road." Carrie patted the street like an idiot. "Not that dirt one." Then she whacked her ears, too. "We *did* fall out . . . must have . . ."

"Where'd the circus go?" Brooke whimpered. "C.C. and Aunt Vira and the circus all went away." Her lip trembled. "I don't feel good."

"I guess . . . C.C. is with the circus," Carrie said slowly. "And the circus is . . . somewhere."

"Where?" Brooke demanded. "Where did it go?"

"I don't know." Carrie shook her head. Then she pulled her knees up to her chin and stared back at the corner where it all had happened. "I don't know," she said again.

Josh thumped his ears for the third time. "Well," he said slowly, "C.C. will like it at the circus." He grinned then. "They sell cotton candy."

"Dummy. Ghosts don't eat." But even as I said it, I could picture C.C. sitting in some circus tent or swinging on some trapeze, stuffing her face with the pink stuff that was about as airy as she was. A half giggle slipped out, like a hiccup.

Josh patted me on the shoulder. "It's been too much for him."

That made me giggle again. Was it that light-headed, floating feeling that made everything seem so funny all of a sudden? I could almost see Aunt Vira sitting all straight and proper at the wheel of the bookmobile, rolling around some circus ring and saying: "When the going gets tough, the tough get going. He who hesitates is lost."

Whether that long-ago circus knew it or not, it was haunted.

"I know what happened!" A sudden smile spread over Brooke's dirty face. "I know why C.C. disappeared. She must be the wart fairy. Fairies are magic."

"C.C. the w-wart fairy!" The giggles bubbled up faster. Now Josh was laughing, too.

"The wart fairy! I love it! A wart fairy in a circus parade!"

"Well, she *could* be. Fairies can disappear," Brooke shouted at him stubbornly.

I doubled over. I pounded my fist in the street.

Everything was funny. The whole afternoon was hilarious.

"What about the kid at the schoolhouse?" Josh gasped through his giggles. "What do you suppose he thought we were?" He flapped his arms up and down. "I am the ghost of . . . of . . . schoolhouse future!" he moaned. "And I've come to suck your blood." He doubled up, choking.

"I've come to suck your blood. I've come to suck your blood." Brooke made a song out of it, spinning around at the edge of the road.

A horn honked. A semi stopped beside us. It must have just turned the corner. The driver leaned out the window.

"What do you kids think you're doing, rolling around practically in the road? You crazy or something? This is a dangerous intersection! You could get in an accident!"

"An accident? In this intersection?" Josh choked, scooting back off the road. "Then we'd be—"

"Ghosts!" I rolled off into the side ditch, clutching my stomach. Tears rolled down my cheeks.

And we all howled.

23

The distance between the schoolhouse and the intersection of Appleridge and Highway 12 was a lot longer on foot than in a speeding ghost bus. By the end of the first mile, Brooke had stopped giggling and started blubbering. The rest of us had to take turns carrying her.

Nothing ever looked as welcome as the sight of Bill's old car clanking down the road with Norbert's head leaning out the front window.

"You kids want a ride?"

"Do we ever!"

"You'll have to squeeze a bit. Bill and me just picked up our old friend Harry from the bus station." Norbert nodded toward the back seat. A thin, wrinkled old man moved over to make room as we all piled in.

"Harry came up from Chicago for the class reunion banquet," Norbert said cheerfully.

It was hard to believe that the man scrunched up in the corner ever could have been anybody's classmate. He looked like the kind of person born in a neatly pressed suit with thin, slicked-down hair and a dried-up apple head.

"These folks are fixin' up the old schoolhouse so you'd hardly know the place," Norbert chatted.

The old man sat up a little straighter. "The schoolhouse? They're *living* in the old schoolhouse?" He stared at us in surprise. "Well, if that doesn't beat all."

"See for yourself," Norbert said, waving his arm toward our lot as Bill swung into the driveway. "You want to take a look around? How many years has it been since you've seen the place?"

"If that doesn't beat all," Harry said again, staring around the yard.

Norbert grinned at him. "Bring back memories?"

Harry got out and stood there, his hands in his pockets.

"The back woods are gone," he said thoughtfully. "And the field. Remember—where we used to play pom-pom-pullaway? And baseball?" He turned to us then, with a smile that brought his wrinkled face to life. "Norbert was quite the baseball champ once upon a time," he said loudly. "Had the best average for miles around."

Norbert drew himself up straighter. "Well, they didn't call me Ty for nothin'," he said. "You've heard of Ty Cobb, haven't you, kids? One of the all-time greats of baseball."

Ty. I jerked away from the old car where I'd been leaning. Ty. I certainly *had* heard the name recently. And . . . the other old guy was . . . *Harry*. . . .

"Remember, over there's where the old pump was and the outhouse and—"

"And over there's where I saw my UFO," Bill cut in with a sideways grin at Norbert. "Remember that, Harry?"

Harry's eyebrows shot up. "Your what?"

"My UFO."

"His little green men. You remember that story, don't you, Harry?" Norbert put his arm around Harry's shoulder. "Bill's UFO he *said* he saw the time he lost our circus money. You haven't forgotten *that*, have you?"

Harry scratched his head. "I remember baseball and marbles, but I sure don't remember any story about UFOs. You pulling my leg, Bill?"

"Well, it was a long time ago. We were just kids—"

"One of us with a *big* imagination—seein' floaty lit-up things—"

Floaty, lit-up things. Harry. Ty. Circus money . . .

Suddenly my head was ringing along like an electric typewriter. Bzzzzzzz, *ding*.

That kid we saw from the bus—the one with the funny cap and knee pants—the one who *dropped*

142

something—that kid was—could have been—Bill.

Someone jabbed me. Someone else stepped on my foot.

"Ty! Did you hear him? He said *Ty!*"

"It was *them!* They're the ones!" Carrie hissed from behind her hand.

"Shh! They'll hear you."

"Holy cow," Josh mumbled. He scratched his head, wiggled his lips, then scratched his head again. "You mean *Norbert* and that guy . . . you mean . . . ?" He shook his head. "My brain just turned inside out."

"The clues all fit together." Carrie was still babbling. "Where we found the jar and—"

"Will you *pipe down?*" I said between clenched teeth.

Harry was still gazing across the lot, hands in his pockets.

"Nope, I just don't remember anything about it," he said again, shaking his head.

Well, he was in his seventies, after all. And he didn't look like the kind who would remember—things.

But Bill did. Bill remembered seeing a strange, floaty thing coming at him, a long time ago, right here in the schoolyard. Something that *wasn't* a UFO and *didn't* have little green men inside—if he only knew. . .

"Well, would you look at that?" Norbert called, peeking through the car window. "I wondered why it was so quiet around here. Little Brooke's fallen asleep in the car." He opened the car door and picked her up. She opened one eye.

"Bye, C.C.," she mumbled sleepily.

"Little Brooke must have had a long day," Norbert said in a whisper.

"Long day." Josh plopped down in the dirt with a long drawn out sigh. "A very long day." He gave his ears another whack. "Seems like years went by."

24

Captain's Log: Stardate July 10, Friday:

*I think we really are living in a
Black Hole—with a time warp.*

I think we fell through it yesterday.

Dad pulled himself up from the dirt and untangled
the fish line from around his ankle. "All right," he
called out in a very calm, controlled voice, "which one
of you kids tied fish line all over the yard?"

"Me." Brooke put her finger in her mouth. "I was
playing spider. The fish line was my web."

"Well, you just untie your web from all the places
you put it, you hear?" He'd gotten his breath back.
His voice wasn't slow or calm anymore. "Here I try
to set aside one day, just one day, for rest and relax-

ation, and I spend it falling on my face. Get moving, young lady!" he thundered.

Brooke couldn't have run away any faster if she had been a daddy longlegs. She didn't get yelled at very often.

Dad brushed himself off, still muttering. "Yesterday it was ghosts and circuses. Today it's spiders." He strode across the yard to Mom. "Lynn, that child has got to find friends her own age. She's living in a dream world!"

"She'll find plenty of friends when school starts. She just has a very active imagination. All of them do, you know."

"Yeah, I know." Dad looked up at the three of us in the oak tree. "And I suppose you three are playing bird and building a nest that attacks people?"

"Just a tree house, Dad." I tried to sound reassuring. "That's all."

"It won't attack anyone. Promise," Josh yelled down.

Dad threw up his hands. "Ask them to help when you're building something, and they gripe and gripe. Ask them to take the day off—and they spend it building." He plopped into the lawn chair and held up his organic gardening magazine like a shield between him and the rest of us.

Poor Dad. He would never understand. After a day like yesterday, we couldn't just lie around in lawn chairs and read until it was time to go to the carnival. There was so much to talk about! It wasn't just every day that ghosts got freed from haunt patterns. It wasn't just every day that kids got to travel into the past and crash into a circus parade. We had plans to make, things to do. We needed our own private place to talk.

And so—the tree house. We'd already spent most of the morning on it. It was almost finished. A plank across the big crotch, a rope pulley for hauling things up, and a box for keeping supplies. With all the leaves for camouflage, we'd have plenty of privacy.

"It's finally getting built," Carrie said, gazing around happily. "My tree house."

"*Our* tree house," I reminded her.

"This is just the kind of stuff Caddie did with *her* brothers. And Trixie Belden, too."

Brooke walked over to the tree. "Can I be in your club?" she yelled up. "I'm not a spider anymore. I threw away my web."

"You can be mascot," I yelled down.

"What do mascots do?"

"They stay on the ground."

She didn't give up. "What's the name of your club?"

"Almost lunchtime," Mom called from the school-house at the same time. She started to go back in, then turned around again.

"Ryan," she called, "don't you think it's about time you took this dirty sign down?" She pointed to my sign above the door. It was faint, but still readable: *THE BLACK HOLE*.

The sign did look pretty grubby beside the new

trim paint. And even though there was still tons of work to do, the schoolhouse didn't look much like a black hole anymore with the new windows and all. Still, I kind of liked the old sign.

"What's the name of your club?" Brooke yelled again.

I looked at Brooke, then over at the sign.

There was a better place for my sign.

Ten minutes later, it was nailed to the tree branch below the tree house with an arrow pointing up.

"What did you put that there for?" Josh put his hands on his hips, frowning.

"Wait." I ran for the can of paint and the brushes hanging at the back of the house. It was hard to do letters with a wide brush, but I managed a sloppy G-A-N-G at the edge of the sign: *THE BLACK HOLE GANG*.

"They met here, too," I said. "The gang. *You* know." I raised my eyebrows at him. "Harry, John, Ty, and Wil. He's Bill. Norbert's gang."

"The Black Hole Gang." Carrie read it slowly, then she smiled. "Yeah. Them and us. Same schoolhouse. Same tree."

It was a neat old tree. It made me feel connected to all the kids who'd climbed it and sat under it during their recesses. Kids with funny knee pants and lard pails with bean sandwiches and comics about Buck Rogers.

Weird. Even back when all they had were those funny-looking early airplanes, kids like Bill were already thinking about spaceships. He had Buck Rogers—and I had Captain Kirk. Kids weren't so different then, really.

Carrie plopped down on the grass. "It all fits. Every single clue," she said with a satisfied nod. "Bill was the kid who saw us coming in Pegasine. He must have dropped the jar when he ran away. It was lost until we came along."

"But we don't have the coins or the ad anymore, thanks to Brooke," I reminded them. They were still inside the bus, back in that long-ago circus.

"They could bring them back," Josh said.

I stared at him. "What do you mean? Who could?"

"C.C. and Aunt Vira. They're lib-er-ated. They got past the intersection and now they can go anywhere they want. Maybe even any *time* they want. They're ghosts, after all."

"Hey, wait a minute." Carrie suddenly sat up straight, frowning. "I just thought of something. When we scared Bill and he dropped the jar with the poster and coins— *we* had the *same* poster and coins *inside* the bus—*at the same time!*"

Josh frowned, too. "Yeah, you're right," he said slowly. He turned to me. "How could the coins and poster be in two places at the same time?"

"But it *wasn't* the same time," I argued. "We found *our* jar this summer—in *our* time. The jar Bill was holding was in *his* time: nineteen twenty-seven. We just *saw* his time. We visited. Get it?"

"I . . . think so." Carrie sounded uncertain. Josh kept staring, eyebrows puckered. I could practically see the wheels turning in his brain. He shook his head finally and flopped on his back with a groan. "That's worse than a full page of math problems."

"Hey, everybody, we got some mail." Brooke ran across the yard, waving something in the air. "I found this in the mailbox. Who's it for?"

"Let me see." I grabbed for it. My fingers closed around something that felt more like leather than paper.

"What's this?" I held it closer. It *was* leather, with a big red flower painted on one side. I flipped it over. The words *POST CARD* were sort of burned into the leather. The date was scrawled off to the side—*1907*? And below that—my breath snagged. In thin, scraggly print were four names: *Ryan, Carrie, Josh, and the Oreo.* Oreo. There were only two people who had heard that name. . .

"What is it? Who's it for?" Josh and Carrie were both trying to see over my shoulder.

"Oreo," Josh said incredulously. "Oreo?" Then, with a low whistle, "Holy cow!"

"C.C.," Carrie breathed. "It's from C.C.! Has to be!"

Josh stabbed his finger down on the date. "See? What'd I tell you—nineteen oh-seven! They *can* go anywhere!"

"But what's it say?" Carrie cried impatiently.

"There's just an ugly flower on the back." I flipped it again.

"It *has* to say something!"

"There!" Carrie squealed, pointing to the edge of the stem. "There's some writing! It *does* say something!"

Our heads knocked together as we bent over the card, staring at the thin, wiggly ink scrawls. They began to form words.

I grinned. So did Carrie. And Josh. We stood there in the yard, smiling at each other and at the leather card with its ghostly scrawl curled like leaves around the stem of the flower.

Three words: *We shall return.*

About the Author

KATHY KENNEDY TAPP lives in Wisconsin with her husband and three children. She works in the children's department of her local library and is an active member of a volunteer puppet group, for which she writes scripts, makes puppets, and puppeteers.

Ms. Tapp's first book for young readers, *Moth-kin Magic*, was a Junior Literary Guild selection. She took her inspiration for *The Ghostmobile* from an old brick schoolhouse down the road from her family's country home. The schoolhouse "haunted" her for a number of years before the story it held developed into the realistic fantasy of this book.